MARVEL CINEMATIC UNIVERSE
PHASE ONE

MARVEL
THE AVENGERS

MARVEL CINEMATIC UNIVERSE
PHASE ONE

MARVEL

THE AVENGERS

Adapted by ALEX IRVINE

Based on the Screenplay by JOSS WHEDON

Story by ZAK PENN and JOSS WHEDON

Produced by KEVIN FEIGE

Directed by JOSS WHEDON

LITTLE, BROWN AND COMPANY
New York   Boston

Little, Brown and Company

Hachette Book Group
1290 Avenue of the Americas, New York, NY 10104
Visit us at lb-kids.com

Little, Brown and Company is a division of Hachette Book Group, Inc.
The Little, Brown name and logo are trademarks of Hachette Book Group, Inc.

The publisher is not responsible for websites (or their content)
that are not owned by the publisher.

First Edition: March 2015

ISBN: 978-0-316-25637-7

10 9 8 7 6 5 4 3 2 1

RRD-C

PRINTED IN THE UNITED STATES OF AMERICA

CHAPTER 1

Nick Fury should have been on the Helicarrier handling his responsibilities as director of S.H.I.E.L.D. The world was full of threats, and the Phase 2 defense initiative required all his attention. Instead, he was stepping off a helicopter in the New Mexico desert, with his right-hand agent, Maria Hill, right behind him.

Another of his most trusted agents, Phil Coulson, met them on the landing pad. The massive S.H.I.E.L.D.

research base loomed around them. It was a hive of activity, with low-level alarms sounding and an automated voice echoing over loudspeakers: *"All personnel, evacuation order has been confirmed. This is not a drill."*

"How bad is it?" Fury asked, raising his voice over the beating rotors of the helicopter.

"That's the problem, sir," Coulson said. "We don't know."

He got them up to speed as they rode the elevator down into the subterranean lab complex where S.H.I.E.L.D. had been housing the artifact known as the Tesseract. During World War II, Hydra had tried to use it to power doomsday weapons. Later, Tony Stark's father, Howard, one of S.H.I.E.L.D.'s founders, had recovered it. Ever since, S.H.I.E.L.D. had been trying to understand its secrets.

Last year, they had made a breakthrough with the assistance of Dr. Erik Selvig, an astrophysicist who had crossed paths with S.H.I.E.L.D. when his protégé Jane Foster had encountered a being from another world. The individual called himself Thor, after the thunder god of Norse mythology—and, after what had happened following Thor's arrival on Earth, Nick Fury believed he was legitimate. Whatever this being's true origin, he had a powerful hammer and he came from a place called Asgard...and he had formidable enemies who'd followed him to Earth.

Those enemies were gone, but Fury had learned his lesson. S.H.I.E.L.D. could no longer focus only on threats coming from Earth. They had to be ready for threats coming from anywhere in the universe.

That was why they'd brought Dr. Selvig in to study the Tesseract. If they could harness its power...

"Dr. Selvig read an energy surge from the Tesseract four hours ago," Coulson was saying.

"I didn't approve going to testing," Fury said.

Coulson nodded. "He wasn't testing it. He wasn't even in the room. Spontaneous event."

"It just turned itself on?" Hill sounded skeptical.

Fury, as usual, was less interested in how they'd gotten there than in what they were going to do next. "What are the energy levels now?"

"Climbing. When we couldn't shut it down, we ordered the evac," Coulson said.

"How long before we get everyone out?"

"Campus should be clear in the next half an hour."

"It better."

Fury and Maria Hill continued on toward the main research area. "Sir," she said as they walked, "evacuation may be futile."

"We should tell them to go back to sleep?"

"If we can't control the Tesseract's energy, there may not be a minimum safe distance."

"I need you to make sure the Phase Two prototypes are shipped out."

"Sir, is that really a priority right now?"

"Until such time as the world ends, we will act as though it intends to spin on. Clear out the tech below. Every piece of Phase Two on a truck and gone."

"Yes, sir." She took some agents with her and headed for the separate area where the Phase 2 prototypes were stored and tested.

Now Fury could focus on Erik Selvig. He stood surrounded by monitors and instruments designed to analyze the forces the Tesseract emitted. "Talk to me, Doctor," he said.

Selvig acknowledged him briefly and then returned his attention to the monitoring equipment. "Director, the Tesseract is misbehaving."

"Is that supposed to be funny?"

"No, it's not funny at all. The Tesseract is not only active, she's . . . *behaving*."

Fury didn't comment on the doctor characterizing the Tesseract as female. He also wasn't interested in Selvig's notions about its personality. It didn't have a personality. It was a cube containing energy, and all Nick Fury wanted was to know how to control that energy. "I assume you pulled the plug."

"She's an energy source. We turn off the power, she turns it back on. If she reaches peak level—"

"We prepared for this, Doctor. Harnessing energy from space."

"We're not ready. My calculations are far from complete. And she's throwing off interference radiation."

Fury watched the Tesseract in its circular containment shell. Eight separate energy sensors built into a frame supporting that shell were designed to measure and conduct that energy. Those sensors in turn rested on stainless-steel support scaffolding. The whole setup sprouted cables and conduits. These were there to supply energy to the Tesseract in a controlled fashion so Dr. Selvig could analyze its reactions. Now they were all shut down, as Dr. Selvig had said, but even so, the Tesseract glowed with a fierce blue energy. It was starting to spill onto the sensors, arcing like electricity. But it wasn't electricity. It was something much more exotic.

"Nothing harmful," Selvig assured him. "Low levels of gamma radiation."

Fury turned slowly to give him a look. "That can be harmful," he said softly. S.H.I.E.L.D. knew of at least one instance where gamma radiation had transformed an ordinary human being, Bruce Banner, into a practically indestructible monster, known as the Hulk. New York City was still recovering from the damage caused getting that one back under control.

"Where's Agent Barton?" he asked.

"The Hawk?" Selvig scoffed, getting Barton's nickname wrong. "In his nest, as usual." He pointed up.

Fury looked where he had pointed but didn't

see anything. "Agent Barton," he said into his mic, "report." All S.H.I.E.L.D. agents and assets wore miniature microphones at all times. Fury was a big believer in communications.

Hawkeye came sliding down a rope from the distant upper reaches of the lab space. When he got to the ground, Fury was already walking. Hawkeye followed. "I gave you this detail so you could keep a close eye on things," Fury said as they moved away from Selvig, leaving him to his work.

"Well, I see better from a distance."

"Have you seen anything that might set this thing off?"

"Doctors," a tech called from near them. "It's spiking again."

"No one's come or gone, and Selvig's clean," Hawkeye said. He and Fury mounted the platform holding the Tesseract's support structure as the cube crackled. "No contacts, no IMs. If there's any tampering, sir, it's not at this end."

Fury shot him a look. "At this end?"

"Yeah, the cube is a doorway to the other end of space, right? Doors open from both sides."

This was true, Fury thought. And he already knew that sometimes unwanted visitors came from space.

Behind him, Selvig cursed and pounded on his keyboard.

From the Tesseract came a fresh blast of energy. Everyone in the complex felt it. Those down in the lab could only watch as a vortex formed around the Tesseract, swirling and glowing. It tightened into a focused beam that shot across the length of the lab and blossomed into a sphere. The same blue energy roiled and sparked on the surface of the sphere. It grew, and the sound of the energy got louder. Inside it was a pure blackness, blotting out the test platform and railings where the sphere had appeared.

Something overloaded, and a wave of energy rolled out from it, flashing across the skin of Fury, Hawkeye, and the assembled scientists. They flinched, but they also wanted to see what was going on....

When the energy faded, a man was left on the platform. He was on one knee with his head tucked into his chest, as if riding out a storm. In the silence, they approached him. The energy blast had scattered equipment and materials across the floor.

The man looked up at them and smiled as he stood. He was not a large man, not remarkable in any particular way. He had long black hair and wore black leather clothing, similar to what Fury was wearing. However, he wasn't a S.H.I.E.L.D. agent. Fury didn't know where he had come from.

Also, the stranger held a kind of spear in his right hand. Set into its head, a gem glowed the same icy blue as the energy that had spilled from the Tesseract.

"Sir," Fury called as armed S.H.I.E.L.D. agents closed nearer, "please put down the spear."

The man looked at the scepter as if he had only just noticed he had it. Then, slowly, he looked back up at Fury, and a vicious smile spread across his face.

He jabbed the scepter in Fury's direction, and a blast of energy from it knocked Fury and Hawkeye back through a bank of monitors and instruments. The S.H.I.E.L.D. agents opened fire, but the bullets didn't seem to hurt the man. He leaped, scepter held high, and cut a path through the agents. In a very short time, the only people left standing in the lab were him and Hawkeye, who had just scrambled back to his feet. Before Hawkeye could unholster and aim his gun, this strange enemy was somehow already across the room. He caught Hawkeye's arm and said softly, "You have heart."

The tip of his scepter touched Hawkeye's chest, not hard enough to hurt him. The gem glowed, and a strange expression came over Hawkeye's face for a moment. He and the stranger looked each other in the eye, and Fury was amazed to see Hawkeye put his gun away.

Now Nick Fury really knew he was up against something…unusual. The only thing he could do was get the Tesseract and try to keep it safe while S.H.I.E.L.D. finished the evacuation and called in some special reinforcements. Tony had to hear about this.

Fury had the Tesseract in a steel carrying case and was taking a step toward the door when the stranger turned to him and said, "Please don't. I still need that."

"This doesn't have to get any messier," Fury said. He glanced quickly around, trying to figure the fastest way out.

"Of course it does," the stranger said. "I've come too far for anything else." He drew himself up a little straighter and said, "I am Loki, of Asgard, and I am burdened with glorious purpose."

"Loki?" Dr. Selvig said. He stood up from helping one of his fellow doctors, who was barely conscious. "Brother of Thor?"

"We have no quarrel with your people," Fury said.

Loki acknowledged Selvig and then returned his attention to Fury. "An ant has no quarrel with a boot," he said.

"Are you planning to step on us?" Fury asked. He already knew this encounter wasn't going to end well, but if he made it out, he needed to know as much about this Loki as possible.

"I come with glad tidings," Loki said. "Of a world made free."

"Free from what?" Fury asked.

Turning back to him, Loki said simply, "Freedom.

11

Freedom is life's great lie. Once you accept that in your heart..." As he spoke the word "heart," he turned and touched Selvig's chest with the tip of his scepter, just as he had with Hawkeye. Selvig gasped, and the same change came over his face that Fury had seen in Hawkeye's. "You will know peace."

No way was Nick Fury going to let this Loki get close enough to do that to him. "Yeah, you say peace," he said, "but I kind of think you mean the other thing."

Hawkeye had been looking around the complex. Now he stepped up to Loki. "Sir, Director Fury is stalling. This place is about to blow and drop a hundred feet of rock on us. He means to bury us."

Loki looked back at Fury, who said, "Like the pharaohs of old."

"He's right, the portal is collapsing in on itself!" Selvig called out from the monitors. "We've got maybe two minutes before this goes critical."

"Well then," Loki said. He glanced over at Hawkeye.

Without a word, Hawkeye drew his gun and shot Nick Fury once, dead center in the chest.

Fury went down without a sound. Loki, Selvig, Hawkeye, and another S.H.I.E.L.D. agent under Loki's control walked quickly out of the lab, Hawkeye carrying the steel briefcase. Inside it, the Tesseract glowed.

CHAPTER 2

Maria Hill saw Hawkeye come out of the lab into the garage with Selvig, a liaison officer, and a stranger carrying a spear. He looked more like one of the people they'd been recruiting into the Avengers Initiative than an ordinary technician or S.H.I.E.L.D. agent. "Who's that?" she asked.

"They didn't tell me," Hawkeye said.

The stranger got into the back of a light armored vehicle. The situation looked suspicious to Hill, but

Hawkeye was one of their most trusted operatives. She wasn't sure what to think.

Then her walkie-talkie crackled. "Hill," came Nick Fury's voice. "Barton has turned!"

She barely had time to dive for cover before Hawkeye was shooting at her. Selvig and the other S.H.I.E.L.D. agent were already in the truck. Hawkeye jumped into another vehicle, and they screeched out of the garage and up the ramp toward the surface. Hill fired after them, but her bullets pinged off the truck's armored exterior.

"They've got the Tesseract!" Fury radioed her. "Shut them down!"

She jumped into a jeep and headed after them. Other S.H.I.E.L.D. vehicles followed, filled with agents. They roared along the underground access road that led up to the surface in the New Mexico desert. She was gaining on them and firing as she drove. Sooner or later, she'd be close enough to have a good shot at the stranger.

He had other ideas, though. When he saw the pursuing convoy get too close, he pointed his scepter at them. The tip of it flared bright blue, and a bolt of energy lashed out from it, striking the vehicle in front of Hill and shattering the right side of its passenger compartment. The vehicle slewed around and flipped, rolling and landing sideways across the road. They were blocked.

At least most of them were. Hill bounced her jeep over a divider into an access road that ran parallel to the road Hawkeye was using. She stood on the gas and hoped she'd be able to cut him off before they got to the surface. Her walkie-talkie was a flurry of voices as Coulson continued to coordinate the evacuation. The energy field they'd created to hold the Tesseract was going to overload very soon.

She heard Coulson's voice: "We're clear upstairs, sir. We need to go." Did that mean Fury had gotten out of the lab? She couldn't stop to find out.

Hill shot out of the side road in front of Hawkeye's car. She yanked her jeep into a reverse slide, spinning it one hundred and eighty degrees so it was suddenly going backward, right in front of Hawkeye. She could see the surprise on his face. She shot at him, shattering both of their windshields. He fired back. Their bumpers met, and both of them nearly lost control—but Hawkeye had more drive going forward, and he forced her out of the way. She spun out, then slammed the jeep back into gear and took off after him again.

The blue orb of the Tesseract containment field collapsed into itself. There was a pause. Then all that energy exploded outward. The entire S.H.I.E.L.D. base heaved and collapsed into itself. The shock wave from the explosion buckled the road. Hill saw Hawkeye's vehicle ahead of the main wave, but she was caught right in it. Debris rained down on the road. She was close to the edge of the base, but she didn't know how much of it was going to collapse from the huge underground crater the explosion had created. She raced forward, hoping she would have enough time.

Fury slammed through the fire doors at the top of the stairs from the laboratory levels. There was a helicopter waiting for him, rotors already spinning. He jumped on, and the helicopter lifted off, just ahead of the shock wave from the explosion. The vehicle carrying Hawkeye and Selvig and Loki—and, more importantly, the Tesseract—roared off into the night. Fury pointed, and the helicopter pilot chased it.

They got around ahead of the truck, and Fury leaned out of the helicopter's side door. He fired, emptying his clip. He could tell from the sparks that some of the bullets had hit, but he was too far away to see if they'd done any damage.

His real target was Loki, but he was protected by the cab of the truck. Fury couldn't get a good shot at him.

Leaning over the truck's roof and keeping low, however, Loki could get a good shot at the helicopter. A blue bolt lanced out and struck the helicopter's rotor assembly. All the control mechanisms went haywire, and the helicopter spiraled down out of the sky. The truck drove underneath them as they were about to crash, close enough that Fury could see the gloating expression on Loki's face.

Fury jumped when they were only twenty feet or so from the ground. He landed hard and rolled, bruising himself pretty well on the rocky ground. The helicopter went over his head and skidded into a crash, its rotors shattering as they spun into the ground. But it didn't explode. He was glad the crew would be safe.

The truck's lights bounced as it drove away across the desert...out of Fury's reach.

"Director." It was Coulson's voice. "Director Fury, do you copy?"

"The Tesseract is with a hostile force. I have men down. Hill?"

Her voice crackled over the radio. She was still in the edges of the collapsed base. "A lot of men still under. I don't know how many survivors."

"Sound a general call," Fury said. "I want every living soul not working rescue looking for that brief-case."

"Roger that," she said.

"Coulson, get back to base. This is a Level Seven," Fury said. He'd never had to say that before, but there was no sense shying away from the truth. Level 7 was S.H.I.E.L.D.'s highest alert status. "As of right now, we are at war."

"What do we do?" Coulson asked after a pause.

Fury knew there was only one answer.

CHAPTER 3

In an abandoned factory next to a rail line in Moscow, Natasha Romanoff sat handcuffed to a chair. In front of her stood the general she'd been assigned to spy on, along with two of his goons. The general stepped up to her and slapped her in the face.

"This is not how I wanted this evening to go," the general said.

Black Widow said nothing. She wasn't afraid. Even if no one on earth knew she was here, even if there was a thirty-foot drop to a concrete floor right behind her, she trusted herself to be able to handle it.

"I know how you wanted this evening to go," she answered in Russian. "Believe me, this is better."

"Who are you working for?" He reeled off some names of his rivals. "Lermontov? Does he think we need to go through him to move goods?"

One of the goons leaned her chair back over the drop. She gasped. "I...I thought General Solohob was in charge of the export business," she said.

The general laughed. "Solohob? A bagman, a front. Your outdated information betrays you. The famous Black Widow, and she turns out to be simply another pretty face."

Natasha pouted at him. "You really think I'm pretty?"

The general smirked and took a few steps away from her, to a table covered with tools. Natasha knew what those were for. She had no intention of letting the general get anywhere near her with them, but she needed him to keep talking. "Tell Lermontov we don't need him to move the tanks. Tell him he is out. Well..." He picked up a torture instrument from the table. Switching to English, he said, "You may have to write it down."

A phone rang.

One of the goons answered in Russian: *"Da?"*

Looking puzzled, he handed the phone to the general. "It's for you."

"You listen carefully," the general growled into the phone—but he was cut off.

Even from her distance, Natasha could hear Agent Coulson's voice. She had extraordinary hearing, part of her...unusual training. "You're at 1-14 Silensky Plaza, third floor," Coulson said, getting right down to business. "We have an F-22 exactly eight miles out. Put the woman on the phone or I will blow up the block before you can make the lobby."

The general's expression changed. Before he had been confident, cocky; now he was surprised that someone had found him...and scared at the thought of a fighter jet with a missile aimed at him.

He put the phone on Natasha's shoulder. Still handcuffed, she pinned it to the side of her head. "We need you to come in," Coulson said.

"Are you kidding? I'm working."

"This takes precedence."

"I'm in the middle of an interrogation. This moron is giving me everything."

The general looked puzzled. "I not...giving everything," he said, looking to his goons. They shrugged.

"Look, you can't pull me out of this right now."

"Natasha, Barton's been compromised."

The words sent a chill down Natasha's spine. *Not Clint...*

She kept her face calm. "Let me put you on hold," she said.

The general reached to take the phone. As he got within range, she jabbed a heel into his knee. With a grunt of pain, he buckled forward, and she headbutted him, making sure he stayed down. Still with the chair on her back and with her hands cuffed behind her, she took out the goons with a quick series of spinning kicks. She even got to use the chair as a weapon, using its legs to smash the second goon's foot and then jumping up in the air to land backward on him, smashing the chair to pieces and knocking him out. The first goon was just getting up after she'd laid him out, and she made sure he stayed down before strolling over to the general. He looked stunned and groggy, but things were about to get worse for him. She wrapped a length of chain around his legs and shoved him off the edge of the drop to the main factory floor. He fell and hung there fifteen feet above the ground. His rivals would find him sooner or later, Natasha thought.

Then she went back to the phone. "Where's Barton now?"

"We don't know."

"But he's alive," she said, trying to make it a statement instead of a question.

"We think so. I'll brief you on everything when you get back. But first you need to talk to the big guy."

"Coulson, you know that Stark trusts me about as far as he can throw me," she said.

"Oh, I've got Stark," Coulson said. "You've got the big guy."

Oh, Natasha thought. *That* big guy. She said something in Russian. It wasn't polite.

CHAPTER 4

Bruce Banner had gotten pretty good at running away and hiding. Once he'd tried it in Brazil and stayed gone for years. Then he'd been forced to come back, when General Ross tried to make him into a weapon. Bruce carried gamma radiation in his blood, and it gave him the power and the curse of changing into the unstoppable green Hulk whenever he lost control of his emotions. The farther he stayed away from the army, and from S.H.I.E.L.D., the more likely he could live a normal life.

Now he was working with the poorest of the poor in a shantytown on the outskirts of Calcutta. The need here was endless, and doctors were few and far between. Bruce did what he could to combat the spread of disease—and also to atone for the damage he'd done when he changed into the Hulk. He had come a long way since then, but he knew the monster always lurked within him, and he had to do whatever was necessary to keep it from taking control. That's what drove him, a desire to be a force for good in the world, despite the Hulk always trying to get out.

Late one night, he was ministering to a sick family, attempting to keep their fevers down without access to advanced medicine, when he heard a commotion at the door. "There is sickness here! Go!" the family's mother said.

Bruce looked and saw a small girl at the door. "You're a doctor?" She spoke English, but repeated the question in Hindi. "My father's sick, and he's not waking up! He has a fever, and he's moaning! But his eyes won't open!"

"Slow down," Bruce said in Hindi. He'd gotten pretty good at picking up languages in his travels.

"My father," she said, begging.

"Like them?" he asked, pointing at the sick children on the bed. They coughed and stirred in their fever.

The little girl just held out one hand with money in it, doubtless everything her family could raise. "Please," she said.

Bruce went with her, ducking away when a jeep full of soldiers passed. She led him into another house, then climbed through a window inside it and disappeared. He stopped on the porch, looking in through the open windows. The house was empty.

A prank? A trap of some kind? Bruce looked around, thinking out loud. "Should have gotten paid up front, Banner," he said.

Then he heard a voice from the shadows where he had just looked. "You know, for a man who's supposed to be avoiding stress, you picked quite a place to settle."

Bruce turned and saw a young woman coming out of the house. She didn't look dressed for a fight. She wore a black dress with a shawl over it and carried no visible weapons.

Bruce didn't know what she wanted, but he figured it wasn't good. She wouldn't have decoyed him all the way out here to the edge of town just to say hello. Anyway, he figured he might as well continue the conversation while he found out. "Avoiding stress isn't the secret," he said.

"Then what is it? Yoga?"

He didn't bother to answer that. "You brought me to the edge of the city," he said. "Smart. I assume the whole place is surrounded?"

"Just you and me."

"And your actress buddy? Is she a spy, too? They start that young?"

She looked him dead in the eye and said, "I did."

"Who are you?"

"Natasha Romanoff."

"Are you here to kill me, Miss Romanoff? Because that's not going to work out for everyone."

"No, of course not. I'm here on behalf of S.H.I.E.L.D."

"S.H.I.E.L.D." Bruce sighed. Some things you just couldn't outrun, he thought. "How did they find me?"

"We never lost you, Doctor. We just kept our distance. Even helped keep some other interested parties off your scent."

"Why?"

"Nick Fury seems to trust you. But now we need you to come in."

"What if I say no?"

"I'll persuade you."

"And what if the other guy says no?'

"You've been more than a year without an incident," she said. "I don't think you want to break that streak."

"Well, I don't get what I want every time," Bruce said, trying not to sound bitter.

Agent Romanoff got more businesslike and direct. "Doctor, we're facing a potential global catastrophe," she said.

"Well, those I actively try to avoid."

She pulled up an image on her phone and put it

down on a low table. "This is the Tesseract. It has the potential energy to wipe out the planet."

He came to look at the image. "What does Fury want me to do—swallow it?"

"He wants you to find it. It's been taken. It emits a gamma signature that's too weak for us to trace. There's no one that knows gamma radiation like you do."

Bruce almost thought she must be joking with him. Gamma radiation had destroyed his life, taken away everything he'd ever had...and now they wanted to exploit how much he knew about it?

"If there was, that's where I'd be," Romanoff added.

"So Fury isn't after the monster," Bruce said. He wanted to be sure what he was getting into.

"Not that he's told me."

"And he tells you everything?"

"Talk to Fury. He needs you on this."

"He's going to put me in a cage?"

"No one's going to put you in a—"

"Stop lying to me!" he roared, slamming his hands

32

on the table. In an eyeblink, she was up and across the room, a gun leveled at Bruce's head.

He felt a little bad when he saw how much he'd terrified her. S.H.I.E.L.D. agents didn't scare easily, but if she'd read Bruce's file, she would have known what he could do. No wonder she was scared. Bruce backed off and gave her a smile. "I'm sorry. That was mean. I just wanted to see what you'd do." What he really wanted was to cut through the song and dance, find out what Nick Fury really wanted and decide whether or not he would go along with it. "Why don't we do this the easy way, where you don't use that and the other guy doesn't make a mess," he said. "Okay? Natasha?"

She lowered the gun. "Stand down," she said, apparently to no one. "We're good here."

Outside, Bruce heard the sound of guns being lowered and hammers uncocked. "Just you and me," he said, quoting Natasha's words back at her to show he knew she was lying. He knew she wouldn't have come alone. Bruce Banner was many things, but stupid wasn't one of them.

CHAPTER 5

Nick Fury had called an emergency meeting of the World Security Council. They needed to know what had happened with the Tesseract, and they needed to know what he planned to do about it. He brought up holographic images of all the WSC members, with their faces and locations hidden. He did not know who they were, but S.H.I.E.L.D. reported to them. He stood in a small room near the Helicarrier's bridge and briefed them on the appearance of Loki and the destruction of the S.H.I.E.L.D. base in New Mexico.

When he was done, they weren't happy. "You're out of line here, Director," one of them said. "You're dealing with forces you can't control."

"You ever been in a war, Councilor? In a firefight? Did you feel an overabundance of control?"

"You're saying that this Asgard has declared war on our planet?"

"Not Asgard," Fury corrected him. "Loki."

Another councilor stepped in. "He can't be working alone. What about the other one? His brother."

"Our intelligence says Thor's not a hostile. But he's worlds away. We can't depend on him to help, either. It's up to us."

"Which is why you should be focusing on Phase Two," said the councilor who had spoken first. "It was designed for exactly this."

"Phase Two isn't ready. Our enemy is. We need a response team."

"The Avengers Initiative was shut down."

"This isn't about the Avengers." That wasn't strictly true, but Nick Fury was no idiot. He wasn't going to show all his cards to the World Security Council when he didn't even know who they were.

"We've seen the list," said a third councilor. "You're running the world's greatest covert security network, and you're going to leave the fate of the human race to a handful of freaks."

"I'm not leaving anything to anyone. We need a response team. These people may be isolated, unbalanced even, but I believe with the right push they can be exactly what we need."

"You believe?" echoed the third councilor.

The first added, "War isn't won by sentiment, Director."

"No," Fury agreed. "It's won by soldiers."

Then he waited to see what they would say. More accurately, he waited for them to say what he had known they would say all along. They did not forbid him from going forward, but Fury knew he couldn't count on them for support, either. He was on his own.

That was all right. Usually he preferred it that way. As long as the Council didn't start going behind his back, he would be fine.

CHAPTER 6

Steve Rogers pounded and pounded on the punching bag that hung from the gym's ceiling. He came here when all else failed—when he was out of options for how to deal with all the information he'd been having difficulty processing. When he had been Captain America, fighting Hydra in Europe during World War II, he'd had a sense of purpose. Now, after seventy years on ice, he was completely adrift. S.H.I.E.L.D. kept him on a short leash, helping him to get used to his sudden appearance in the year 2012. But it didn't always work, and sometimes the only way Steve could stop himself from going crazy was to get into the gym and hit the bag.

He thought of his fellow soldiers and hit the bag. He thought of Peggy Carter and slammed it again. He thought of Howard Stark, of progress, advancement, of the seventy years of history he'd not been a part of, and he punched and punched: harder and harder, faster and more furious.

He remembered the battle aboard the Red Skull's plane. Like it was yesterday, he saw the energies of the cube open a hole in space and suck the Red Skull through. He remembered the moment when he knew he wouldn't be able to stop the Hydra superweapons from destroying New York City . . . and he knew he'd have to crash the plane. He knew he would have to sacrifice himself to save millions. He remembered saying good-bye to Peggy. . . .

Then he remembered waking up, in this strange future New York where he was a man out of time. He didn't belong here, in present day. Everyone he knew was gone or too old to remember him. Peggy, Bucky…everyone. But he was still here, and all he could do was try to sort things out because Steve Rogers was Captain America. People were counting on him.

His punches built to a rage, and a final haymaker tore the heavy bag loose from its moorings and knocked it across the gym. It lay there spilling sand on the floor.

Steve was barely breathing hard. He wasn't done. He went and picked up another bag. He had a row of them ready for when he got in these moods, and all he wanted to do was hit something.

As he hung the new bag from the chain, he heard Director Fury's voice. "Trouble sleeping?"

"I slept for seventy years, sir," Steve said. He started a new series of punches, trying to find a nice easy rhythm. "I think I've had my fill."

"Then you should be out celebrating. Seeing the world," Fury said.

Steve stopped. He could tell Fury wanted to talk

to him about something, so he started stripping the workout tape from his fists. "When I went under, the world was at war," he said. "I wake up, they say we won. They didn't say what we lost."

Fury nodded. He and Steve had talked about this before. He knew Steve was having trouble getting used to his new environment. "We've made some mistakes along the way. Some very recently."

Steve cut to the chase. "Are you here with a mission, sir?"

"I am."

"Trying to get me back in the world?"

"Trying to save it," Fury said. He handed Steve a dossier. Steve opened it and on the first page saw a picture of the Red Skull's cube under the heading TESSERACT. "Hydra's secret weapon," he said.

"Howard Stark fished that out of the ocean when he was looking for you," Fury explained. "He thought what we think. The Tesseract could be the key to unlimited sustainable energy. That's something the world sorely needs."

"Who took it from you?" Steve asked, handing the dossier back. There was nothing in it he needed if he was going to get a briefing from Fury.

Fury hesitated. "He's called Loki. He's...not from around here. There's a lot we'll have to bring you up to speed on if you're in. The world has gotten even stranger than you already know."

"At this point, I doubt anything would surprise me."

"Ten bucks says you're wrong. There's a debriefing packet waiting for you back at your apartment."

Steve picked up a heavy bag to take home, but Fury wasn't quite ready to let him go just yet. "Is there anything you can tell us about the Tesseract that we ought to know now?" he asked.

Steve remembered the power of the cube. He'd seen it tear a hole in space and suck the Red Skull through. It wasn't something to mess around with. "You should have left it in the ocean," Steve said.

Then he went home, to hang the heavy bag there and try one more time to punch his nightmares away.

But he and Fury both knew he wasn't bailing out on the mission. Steve knew all too well the destruction that could be wrought if the power of the cube fell into the wrong hands. He'd seen the destruction it caused when the Red Skull held it and used it to power new weapons. What if someone smarter and more dangerous got hold of it? No matter what Steve was struggling with, if the world needed Captain America, he would rise to meet the challenge.

CHAPTER 7

The New York City skyline glittered. The bridges sparkled like diamonds in the reflective waters of the East River. In recent years, the city had been built back up from darker days at the turn of the millennium. But even with the explosion of construction the metropolis was experiencing, one tower was sure to stand out above all the others.

Like a cannon fired from a submarine, Iron Man shot from below the surface of the river and soared into the sparkling sky over Manhattan. "Good to go on this end," he said. "The rest is up to you."

"You disconnected the transmission lines?" Pepper asked. "Are we off the grid?"

"Stark Tower is about to become a beacon of self-sustaining clean energy," Tony said. That was what he'd been doing on the bottom of the river—routing the city electrical supply around the feeder conduits that powered the new Stark Tower.

"Well, assuming the Arc Reactor takes over and it actually works," Pepper pointed out.

The PR campaign had been a success, the media outlets were alerted, and Stark Industries' CEO was ready to flip the switch. Tonight was the night they lit Stark Tower—New York's newest and most spectacular skyscraper, and its most eco-friendly: the first in not just the city, but the world to run on self-sustaining energy.

Tony rocketed low over Fifth Avenue, heading north. "I assume," he said. "Light 'er up."

In the penthouse apartment on top of the new Stark Tower, Pepper hit a switch. The tower began to light up, first from street level, and then hundreds of feet to the pinnacle, illuminating the New York skyline—and the sky itself.

"How does it look?" Pepper asked. He could see her grinning with excitement in the heads-up display inside the helmet of his Iron Man suit.

"Like Christmas, but with more me," Tony said.

"We've got to go wider on the public awareness campaign," she said, thinking like the CEO she was. The best decision Tony had ever made was handing the reins of Stark Industries over to her. "You need to do some press. I'm in DC tomorrow working on the zoning for the next three buildings...."

"Pepper, you're killing me," Tony said as he arced past the Empire State Building. "The moment, remember? Enjoy the moment."

"Get in here and I will," she said.

He landed on the rooftop of Stark Tower, aiming for a landing pad and walkway specially constructed for Iron Man. As he walked toward the penthouse office and living space he shared with Pepper, machines automatically removed the Iron Man armor piece by piece. Tony didn't even have to break stride. He sure had come a long way since the first time he'd built one of the suits in a cave in Afghanistan. Then he'd been trying to save his life. Now he could maybe save the world.

"Sir, Agent Coulson of S.H.I.E.L.D. is on the line for you," Jarvis said through the communications line in Tony's helmet.

"I'm not in," Tony said. A machine removed the Iron Man helmet. "I'm actually out," he added. He knew Jarvis would make an excuse for him. That was one of the things he'd programmed into Jarvis, who was his very own artificial intelligence, technological consultant, and butler. There was no way he was going to spoil this evening by dealing with Coulson. He had something to celebrate.

"Sir," Jarvis said via one of the speakers set into the suit disassembly systems. "I'm afraid he's insisting."

"Grow a spine, Jarvis," Tony said. "I got a date."

By the time he got inside, he was wearing ordinary clothes. Pepper stood watching a holographic display of Stark Tower and the Arc Reactor powering it. "Levels are holding steady, I think," she said.

"Of course they are. I was directly involved. Which brings me to my next question. How does it feel to be a genius?"

"Well, I really wouldn't know, now would I?" Pepper teased him.

He poured two glasses of champagne and they toasted. "What do you mean? All this came from you."

"No, all this came from that." Pepper tapped the miniaturized Arc Reactor in Tony's chest.

"Give yourself some credit, please. Stark Tower is your baby. Give yourself...twelve percent of the credit."

"Twelve percent."

Tony had meant it as a joke, but he could see she hadn't taken it that way. "An argument could be made for fifteen," he said, trying to get a laugh out of her.

It wasn't working. "Twelve percent," she said. "My baby."

Now he decided to tease her a little more. "Well, I

did do all the heavy lifting. Literally, I lifted the heavy things. I'm going to pay for that comment about percentages, in some subtle way later, aren't I?"

"It's not going to be that subtle."

"I'll tell you what. The next building is going to say Potts on the tower."

"On the lease," she corrected him.

"Sir, the telephone," Jarvis said. "I'm afraid my protocols are being overridden."

Coulson's voice came out of the speaker on Tony's dining room table, where he and Pepper had been just about to enjoy their champagne. "Mr. Stark, we need to talk."

"You have reached the life model decoy of Tony Stark," Tony said, trying to get Coulson to leave them alone. "Please leave a message."

"This is urgent."

"Then leave it urgently."

The elevator door opened, revealing Coulson hanging up his phone.

"Security breach," Tony said to Pepper. "It's on you."

"Mr. Stark," Coulson began.

Before Tony could say something rude, Pepper greeted Coulson with a big smile. "Phil! Come in."

"Phil?" Tony hadn't even known that was his name. How did Pepper know that?

"I can't stay," Coulson said.

"His first name is Agent," Tony protested.

Pepper guided Coulson into the living room, saying, "Come on in. We're celebrating."

"Which is why he can't stay," Tony said.

Coulson held a leather-bound folder out to Tony. "We need you to look this over as soon as possible."

"I don't like being handed things," Tony said. He didn't take the folder.

"That's fine, because I love to be handed things. So let's trade." Pepper took the folder and gave Coulson her champagne. Then she stuck the folder in Tony's hand, took his champagne glass, and helped herself to a sip. "Thank you."

"Official consulting hours are between eight and five every other Thursday," Tony said.

"This isn't a consultation," Coulson said.

"Is this about the Avengers?" Pepper asked. Coulson

gave her a sharp look. "Which I know nothing about," she added. This wasn't true. Tony had told her about the project. He told Pepper everything and didn't care if Coulson knew that or not.

Since the topic of the Avengers had been raised, though, Tony thought he might as well see it through. "The Avengers Initiative was scrapped, I thought. And I didn't even qualify."

"I didn't know that, either," Pepper said.

"Yeah," Tony said. "Apparently I'm volatile, self-obsessed, don't play well with others...."

Pepper was nodding. "That I did know."

"This isn't about personality profiles anymore," Coulson said. He wasn't giving up, and that irritated Tony even more than the fact he'd showed up right when the celebration of Stark Tower was supposed to be starting.

"Whatever," he said. "Ms. Potts, got a second?"

She excused herself as Tony opened the files Coulson had given him and started piping them to his desktop display. "You know, I thought we were having a moment," he said.

"I was having twelve percent of a moment," she shot back. "This seems serious. Phil's pretty shaken."

"How would you know if it's serious?" Tony asked.

She ignored the question as she watched the files and images stack up on Tony's virtual desktop. "What is all this?"

"This is…" Tony spread his fingers, and Coulson's files spread across the air above the desktop. One of the new features of Tony's new apartment was a holographic workstation he could spawn from any surface. There were dozens of files: text dossiers, video clips, all kinds of stuff. It was more then they could take in right then.

After a moment, Pepper said, "I'm going to take the jet to DC tonight." She was supposed to be presenting some of Stark Industries' new energy initiatives to a congressional committee tomorrow.

"Tomorrow," Tony said. There was no reason for her to leave tonight. They still owed each other a celebration, whatever Agent Coulson thought.

But Pepper had other ideas. "You have homework,"

she said. She looked at all the images on the display. "A lot of homework."

"Well, what if I didn't?" Tony asked. He gave her a little wink.

She played along. "If you didn't? You mean when you've finished?"

Pepper whispered in his ear and stepped back. Blushing, Tony said, "Square deal. Fly safe."

She kissed him and walked toward the elevator. "Any chance you're driving by the airport?" she asked Coulson.

"I can drop you," he said.

"Fantastic," she said. Then they were gone, and Tony was left with the files. So much for the celebration. There was nothing to do but get to work.

CHAPTER 8

We're about forty minutes out from home base," the Quinjet pilot said. Coulson took off his headphones and made his way back from his station near the cockpit to the passenger compartment. Captain America was sitting there, in civilian clothes, reviewing the dossier Director Fury had given him. After dropping Pepper at the airport, Coulson had stayed up most of the night getting things arranged to have the new team meet for the first time. The logistics were still coming together. He'd picked up Captain America first thing in the morning and was now ferrying him to a meeting with Director Fury.

"So this Dr. Banner was trying to replicate the serum they used on me," Captain America said.

"A lot of people were. You were the world's first Super Hero." Coulson had a bit of a difficult time keeping his normal reserved demeanor around Captain America. He'd been a huge fan for a long time, reading the stories of Captain America's exploits during World War II. Now to see the man right in front of him in the flesh...it was a thrill, but also intimidating. Coulson needed to keep his head. There was a mission to accomplish.

"Banner thought gamma radiation might hold the key to unlocking Erskine's original formula," he added.

"That didn't really go his way, did it?" Captain America was now reading through the part of the dossier containing the history of the Hulk.

"Not so much. When he's not that thing, though, the guy's like a Stephen Hawking."

Captain America looked up at him. He didn't know who Stephen Hawking was.

"He's like a…smart person," Coulson amended. Then, because he couldn't help himself, he went on. "I have to say it's an honor to meet you officially. I sort of met you, I mean I watched you while you were sleeping." Captain America looked uncomfortable, and Coulson regretted his choice of phrase. Captain America got up and looked out the Quinjet's front windows.

Coulson tried again. For some reason, being around Captain America made him nervous in a way he never was when he interacted with any of the others. "I mean, I was present while you were unconscious from the ice," he said. "You know, it's really just a huge honor to have you on board."

"I hope I'm the man for the job," Captain America said.

"Oh, you are. Absolutely. We made some modifications to the uniform." Coulson paused, a little bashful. "I had a little design input."

Captain America looked back at Coulson. "The

uniform? Aren't the Stars and Stripes a little...old-fashioned?"

"With everything that's happening, and the things that are about to come to light, people might just need a little old-fashioned," Coulson said.

Loki watched Dr. Erik Selvig work, preparing the Tesseract for the next phase of his plan. Technicians and soldiers scurried about on various errands. Loki did not know the details and did not care. They were beneath him. He had his eye solely on the greater prize. It was time to consult with the Chitauri and begin the next phase of the preparations.

The gem in the head of his scepter glowed as Loki gathered his magical powers. A moment later, his surroundings were transformed. No longer was he standing in an underground laboratory watching mortals build machines. Now he was sitting in the...other space...where the Chitauri waited.

They were the aliens who had found him after he

was cast out of Asgard. He had struck a deal with them.

Deep space and a field of stars surrounded this rocky world. Pale blue lights glowed where the Chitauri had built their fortress. They gleamed in a set of stairs that climbed to the topmost tower. That was where Loki had made his bargain with the Chitauri: They would be his army and he would open a path to Earth for them. Once Earth was his, and Asgard as well, he would turn the Tesseract over to them.

At least that was what he had promised.

"The Chitauri grow restless," their leader growled. Around him, his minions moved, seemingly part of the rocky landscape until their motion gave them away. They were armored, their faces hidden. They were humanoid in shape, with monstrous faces similar to the reptiles found on Earth. Their appearance would be useful when it was time to use them as an invading army. Striking fear into one's opponents was a fine way to shorten a battle. Loki had also taken care with his own appearance, assuming his

Asgardian armor and horned golden helmet for this conversation. It was useful to appear powerful when you spoke with those you were to lead.

"Let them gird themselves," he said. "I will lead them in glorious battle."

"Battle?" the Chitauri warrior snorted. "Against the meager might of Earth?"

"Glorious," Loki repeated. "Not lengthy. If your force is as formidable as you claim."

He had intended to anger the Chitauri, and he had succeeded. "You question us? You question him, who put the scepter in your hand? Who gave you ancient knowledge and new purpose when you were cast out, defeated?" Thousands of Chitauri warriors watched, their armor scraping on the stones of this strange world.

"I was a king!" Loki declared. "The rightful king of Asgard, betrayed."

"Your ambition is little and born of childish need. We look beyond the Earth to greater worlds the Tesseract will unveil."

"You don't have the Tesseract yet." The Chitauri leader rushed at Loki and stopped just short of him, claws raised. Loki did not move.

"I don't threaten," he said, though he was doing exactly that. "But until I open the doors, until your force is mine to command, you are but words." He wanted the Chitauri to understand that if they wanted the Tesseract, they first had to give Loki what he wanted: Earth.

The Chitauri leader backed down but only a step. "You will have your war, Asgardian," he growled. Then he too decided to make a threat. "If you fail, if the Tesseract is kept from us, there will be no realm, no barren moon, no crevice where he cannot find you. You think you know pain? He will make you long for something as sweet as pain."

Loki flashed back into his awareness of Earth. He took a deep breath. The Chitauri did not frighten him...but he would have been a fool if he had not possessed a healthy respect for their leader, the mad Titan known as Thanos. For it was Thanos who had given Loki the scepter, and Thanos who had rallied the Chitauri to Loki's cause...and Thanos who wished to possess the Tesseract for his own monstrous ends. One did not bargain lightly with Thanos—and one certainly did not fail to meet the terms of such a bargain.

CHAPTER 9

The Quinjet roared in toward the aircraft carrier stationed off the East Coast of the United States. Its pilot brought it in skillfully, using the Quinjet's vertical takeoff and landing capability to bring it down near the command superstructure.

"Stow the captain's gear," Coulson instructed one of the crew members as they disembarked.

A red-haired woman in civilian clothing—with a

sidearm in a holster on her left thigh—was coming across the flight deck to meet them. Coulson introduced them. "Agent Romanoff, Captain Rogers."

"Ma'am." Steve nodded.

"Hi," she said to Steve. To Coulson she added, "They need you on the bridge. They're starting the face trace."

"See you there," Coulson said.

As he left, Agent Romanoff started walking with Steve. "It was quite the buzz around here, finding you in the ice," she said. "I thought Coulson was going to swoon. Did he ask you to sign his Captain America trading cards yet?"

"Trading cards?"

"They're vintage. He's very proud."

Steve saw Bruce Banner looking at one of the S.H.I.E.L.D. fighter jets nearby and called out to him. "Dr. Banner."

Bruce came over and shook his hand. "Yeah, hi. They told me you'd be coming."

"Word is you can find the cube," Steve said.

"Is that the only word on me?" Bruce asked.

Steve knew what his real question was. "Only word I care about," he said. He didn't judge Bruce for what the Hulk had done. All that mattered was whether the scientist could contribute to the mission.

"It must be strange for you, all of this," Bruce said as they walked along the aircraft carrier's flight deck.

"Well, this is actually kind of familiar," Steve said. He was comfortable in a military setting, and he had been on aircraft carriers before. The *Yorktown,* the *Enterprise* . . . a long time ago.

"Gentlemen," Agent Romanoff said. "You might want to step inside in a minute. It's going to get a little hard to breathe."

"Flight crew, secure the deck," a voice said over the ship's speakers.

"Is this a submarine?" Steve asked. He couldn't imagine an aircraft carrier that could operate underwater. How would you seal it? Where would all the planes go? Wouldn't the drag from the water tear up the flight deck and the gun turrets?

"Really?" Bruce said. "They want me in a submerged, pressurized metal container?"

They walked to the edge of the deck and Steve saw he'd had it exactly wrong. The carrier wasn't going down . . . it was going up.

Huge turbines, each fifty yards across, appeared, churning the ocean into froth. Crews ran to lock the planes in place on the flight deck and secure other essential equipment.

"No, this is much worse," Bruce said.

The carrier lifted into the air. Steve couldn't believe what he was seeing. An aircraft carrier that could fly! "Welcome aboard the S.H.I.E.L.D. Helicarrier," Agent Romanoff said. "Now if you'll come with me?"

Steve and Bruce followed her from the flight deck down to the Helicarrier's bridge, which was underwater while it was in naval operation mode. Now it was a glass-walled hive of activity, full of officers and command staff. Steve had a moment to look around. The commanding officer appeared to be a woman with short dark hair reeling off orders from near the center of the bridge. "S.H.I.E.L.D. Emergency Protocol 193.6 in effect," she was saying after a series of status orders and acknowledgments. Steve didn't know what protocol that was. At the moment, all he knew was that he was on a flying aircraft carrier...and wasn't that enough? Amazing.

"We're at level, sir," she said, and that was when Steve saw Nick Fury, at his own station. He was overseeing everything, not interfering, trusting his people to do their jobs.

"Good," he said. "Let's vanish, Agent Hill."

She nodded. "Engage retro-reflection panels."

The Helicarrier disappeared from view. From the inside, it didn't look any different, but Steve saw monitors from satellite feeds, and on those, the Helicarrier had simply become invisible. He corrected himself: He wasn't just on a flying aircraft carrier. He was on an *invisible* flying aircraft carrier.

The future was pretty...cool, was the word everyone used now.

"Gentlemen," Fury said in greeting.

Steve got out his wallet and handed Fury ten dollars. Fury had won the bet fair and square; Steve was in fact surprised by what he was seeing. Not just surprised—astounded. Fury nodded, with just the hint of a smile, and stowed the bill in his pocket.

"Doctor, thank you for coming," he said to Bruce. A crew member at a navigation terminal called out the Helicarrier's altitude: twenty-four thousand feet and climbing toward an operational cruising altitude of thirty thousand.

"Thanks for asking nicely," Bruce said. "So how long am I staying?"

"Once we get our hands on the Tesseract, you're in the wind."

Bruce nodded. "Where are you with that?"

Fury looked to Coulson, who said, "We're sweeping every wirelessly accessible camera on the planet. Cell phones, laptops...if it's connected to a satellite, it's eyes and ears for us."

"That's still not going to find them in time," Agent Romanoff said.

Bruce seemed to agree. "You have to narrow your

field. How many spectrometers do you have access to?"

"How many are there?" Fury asked, meaning that S.H.I.E.L.D. could get access to all of them if necessary.

"Call every lab you know. Tell them to put the spectrometers on the roof and calibrate them for gamma rays. I'll rough out a tracking algorithm basic cluster recognition. At least we can rule out a few places that way." Bruce had taken off his jacket. Now he was rolling up his sleeves. "You have somewhere for me to work?"

"Agent Romanoff?" Fury called. She looked over. "Show Dr. Banner to his laboratory, please?"

"You're going to love it, Doc," she said as she led him off the bridge. "You've got all the toys."

In Loki's hideout, Erik Selvig was receiving a new shipment of supplies and parts. "Put it over there,"

he ordered as a group of technicians wheeled in the crates. He was putting the final touches on the machine Loki had commissioned him to create. "Where did you find all these people?" he asked Barton, who was tapping at a tablet nearby.

"S.H.I.E.L.D. has no shortage of enemies, Doctor," Barton said. "Is this the stuff you need?"

"Yeah, iridium. It's found in meteorites," Selvig explained. "It forms antiprotons. It's very hard to get hold of."

"Especially if S.H.I.E.L.D. knows you need it," Barton commented.

"Well, I didn't know." Barton's comment made Selvig a little defensive. It wasn't like he had planned to need iridium when he'd gone to work in New Mexico three days ago. But he brightened as he saw Loki approach. "Hey, the Tesseract has shown me so much." Selvig struggled to find words that would convey what he had experienced working with the cube. "It's more than knowledge," he said. "It's . . . truth."

"I know," Loki said. "What did it show you, Agent Barton?"

Barton turned to look at Loki. "My next target," he said.

Loki nodded. "Tell me what you need."

Barton took one his bows out of a case and snapped it into shape with a flick of his arm. "I need a distraction," he said. "And a biometric ID."

CHAPTER 10

It took nearly twenty-four hours, but Coulson had finally gotten the courage up to ask Captain America to sign his trading card. "I mean, if it's not too much trouble."

"No, it's fine," Captain America said. He was spending a lot of time on the Helicarrier's bridge, watching how the flight crew operated. He liked to know things like that. You never knew when they would come in handy.

"It's a vintage set. Took me a couple of years to collect them all. Near mint. Slight foxing around the edges, but…"

"We got a hit!" called Agent Jasper Sitwell, one of the S.H.I.E.L.D. officers who worked closely with Fury and Hill. He was in charge of the search for gamma radiation, keyed to the search procedures Bruce had designed. "Sixty-seven percent match. Wait…cross-match…seventy-nine percent."

That was pretty decisive. Either Loki was at that location, or someone else had some of the power of the Tesseract and was carrying it there.

"Location?" Coulson asked.

"Stuttgart, Germany," Sitwell said. "28 König-strasse. He's not exactly hiding."

A map appeared on one of the monitors close to Coulson and Captain America. That address looked to be a museum of some kind, facing a large open plaza. There would be lots of civilians. A tricky place to operate…but they didn't have a choice.

"Captain," Fury said, "you're up."

The benefit at the museum in Stuttgart was quite a high-end affair. A string quartet played for the gathered donors and local celebrities, who milled around in their best clothes making small talk. Outside, Barton infiltrated security without breaking stride. He handed off his bow to a member of his support team and cracked the side door's access panel.

Inside, Loki had been mingling with the crowd, taking on the appearance of an ordinary man with a walking stick. But as the president of the museum, one Doktor Heinrich Schäfer, began his welcoming speech, Loki decided it was time to make a dramatic entrance. He tapped the walking stick on the floor and it became his scepter. Immediately, to get the crowd's attention, he aimed it at the nearest museum security guard and fired. Screams echoed through the vaulted museum lobby. Loki strode the rest of the way down the stairs and manhandled Schäfer over to a stone altar that was one of the museum's prized ancient Norse relics. He slammed Schäfer onto his back, forcing a machine over his face. Schäfer cried out in pain and surprise as the machine shone blinding light into his face, holding his eyes open.

Outside, Barton held a portable holographic projector over the access panel. A three-dimensional model of Doktor Schäfer's eye appeared in the projector field. The door opened.

Inside, people screamed and fled the sudden violence. Loki strode through the museum's great hall, his appearance transforming. He had walked in wearing a suit and tie like everyone else. Now he was garbed in the cloak and armor of his Asgardian heritage. The twin horns of his helmet gleamed in the streetlights as he followed the crowd outside. A police car, alerted by the commotion, raced toward him. He blasted it with his scepter, and it spun out of control and crashed.

The crowd had clustered in the plaza in front of the museum. Loki willed himself to be in their midst, and he was, appearing magically to stop them from fleeing any farther. "Kneel before me," he commanded.

They scattered away from him. Loki multiplied himself, creating illusions that looked just like him all over the plaza. "I...said...KNEEL!" he roared, and the sound came from all of the copies of him as well, booming through the open space.

The crowd froze. Slowly the crowd knelt, and Loki reveled in their submission. "There," he said. "Is this not simpler? Is this not your natural state? It's the unspoken truth of humanity, that you crave subjugation. The bright lure of freedom diminishes your life's joy in a mad scramble for power, for identity. You were made to be ruled. In the end, you will always kneel."

An old man in the middle of the crowd stood. Loki paused in his speech to regard this individual. Around him, all the copies of himself also looked at this old man.

"Not to men like you," the old man said.

"There are no men like me," Loki said.

"There are always men like you," the old man said.

."Look to your elder, people," Loki said. "Let him be an example." A wolfish grin spread over his face, and he leveled the scepter at the old man.

As the blast discharged from it, someone dropped from the sky and blocked it with a shield! The bolt of energy reflected back and knocked Loki down.

Loki looked up to see a muscular costumed hero, wearing blue with stripes of white and red. His shield was also decorated in those colors, with a five-pointed star at its center that matched the star on the hero's chest. "You know," he said, "the last time I was in Germany and saw a man standing above everybody else, we ended up disagreeing."

"The soldier," Loki spat. He knew of this one. The so-called Captain America. He got to his feet. "The man out of time."

"I'm not the one who's out of time," Captain America said. There was an engine whine, and a Quinjet hovered into view over the plaza. From its belly hung a mounted gun.

Agent Romanoff's voice came over the Quinjet's speakers: *Loki, drop the weapon and stand down.*

76

Instead, Loki fired a blast from the scepter at the Quinjet, which rolled out of the way. Captain America flung his shield, striking Loki in the arm and knocking him briefly off balance. The shield returned to him, and he followed it up with a right cross to Loki's jaw.

But Loki was tougher than he looked. He struck back with the scepter, forcing Captain America to parry until Loki found an opening and slammed the butt of the scepter into Captain America's midsection, knocking him down. Captain America threw the shield again, but this time Loki was ready. He knocked it aside. It fell ringing to the stones of the plaza, and Loki had the tip of the scepter against the back of Captain America's neck before the soldier could get back to his feet.

"Kneel," he said.

Captain America pivoted into a leaping spinning kick that knocked Loki flat. "Not today," he said.

The battle was rejoined as Agent Romanoff tried to maneuver the Quinjet into position for a clean shot at Loki. "Guy's all over the place," she complained. She couldn't fire without possibly hitting either Captain America or one of the bystanders running all over the plaza.

Her communications system squawked, and she heard a familiar song…and a familiar voice. "Agent Romanoff. You miss me?"

It was Tony Stark.

The music blared over the Quinjet's speakers, echoing through the plaza, as Iron Man blazed down out of the sky. A twin blast from his repulsor gauntlets smashed Loki to the ground. Iron Man landed and made a show of deploying every weapon the Iron Man suit had: repulsors, minimissiles, unibeam, the whole works. "Make your move, Reindeer Games," he said.

Loki didn't move. He returned to his civilian appearance and held up his hands.

"Good move," Iron Man said. He retracted all of his armaments.

Captain America came up next to him. "Mr. Stark."

"Captain."

CHAPTER 11

They stood guard over Loki on the Quinjet, getting him back to the Helicarrier as quickly as possible. Loki said nothing and offered no further resistance. Captain America leaned in close to Tony Stark and said, "I don't like it."

"What—Rock of Ages giving up so easily?"

Steve snorted. "I don't remember it being that easy. This guy packs a wallop."

"Still, you're pretty spry for an older fellow," Tony

said. "What's your thing—Pilates? Oh, right. That's kind of like calisthenics. You must have missed a lot while you were doing time as a Capsicle."

Steve didn't take the bait. He knew Tony liked to get under people's skin. All he said was, "Fury didn't tell me he was calling you in."

"Yeah, there're a lot of things Fury doesn't tell you."

A sudden storm rose around the Quinjet. Natasha looked at the instrument panel. There'd been no warning of heavy weather. "Where's this coming from?" she wondered out loud.

At first, she thought that Loki was responsible. But that didn't appear to be the case. He looked more nervous than anyone else on the jet.

"What's the matter?" Cap asked. "You scared of a little lightning?"

"I'm not overly fond of what follows," Loki replied.

A loud crack of thunder punctuated Loki's remark, and soon after, the Quinjet rocked as something huge landed on top of the jet. Captain America and Iron Man suited up, preparing to respond. From a jet cam, Natasha could see a man in full battle armor

crouching on top of the jet, illuminated by the lightning that crashed around him. He had long blond
hair and held a square-headed hammer.

Iron Man punched the button that lowered the rear
gangway of the Quinjet. Turbulence rocked the plane,
and the wind inside swirled wildly. "What are you
doing?" Steve shouted over the tempest.

As the ramp got all the way open, the hammer-
bearing attacker appeared on the gangway.

Stunned, Iron Man held up his hands to fire a repulsor blast, but before he could act, the hammer hit him
square in the gut, knocking him into Captain America
and tangling both of them in a heap up front near the
cockpit. With Iron Man and Captain America out of
commission, the blond warrior grabbed Loki around
the neck, and before anyone could do anything about
it, he raised the hammer and jumped back out of the
Quinjet, disappearing into the storm.

"Another Asgardian?" Natasha called from the
cockpit.

"That guy's a friendly?" Steve asked. It was hard to
believe.

"Doesn't matter," Iron Man said. "If he frees Loki—or kills him—the Tesseract's lost."

"Stark, we need a plan of attack!" Steve said as Iron Man stomped toward the open gangway.

"I have a plan," Iron Man said over his shoulder. "Attack."

Then he rocketed out of the ship.

Steve was amazed at the speed at which Tony moved. He grabbed a parachute and strapped it on.

Natasha looked at him skeptically. They were thousands of feet above land, the Quinjet was moving at a supersonic clip, and—as far as she knew—Captain America couldn't fly.

"I'd sit this one out, Cap," she said.

"I don't see how I can," Steve said.

"These guys come from legend. They're basically gods."

Maybe Steve was old-fashioned, but he didn't think so. "There's only one God, ma'am. And I'm pretty sure he doesn't dress like that."

Then he took three steps to the edge of the gangway, gauged the Quinjet's slipstream, and jumped.

Thor let Loki fall well before they got to the ground. Loki's impact dug up a trench on the forested hillside, and he lay groaning while Thor landed near him. "Where is the Tesseract?"

With a pained laugh, Loki said, "I missed you, too."

"Do I look to be in a gaming mood?"

"You should thank me," Loki said. He was starting to get up. "With the Bifrost gone, how much dark energy did the All-Father have to muster to conjure you here, to your precious Earth?"

Thor dropped Mjolnir and caught his brother by the shirtfront, giving him a quick but powerful shake. "I thought you were dead," he growled.

"Did you mourn?"

"We all did. Our father—"

"*Your* father," Loki replied. He swatted Thor's hands away, and Thor let him. "He did tell you my true parentage, did he not?"

"Loki, we were raised together. We played together; we fought together. Do you remember *none* of that?"

"I remember a shadow," Loki said bitterly. "Living in the shade of your greatness. I remember you tossing me into an abyss. I who was and should be king!"

Because you would have destroyed Asgard, Thor thought. *Just to impress our father, you would have annihilated all the Nine Realms.* "So you took the world I love as recompense for your imagined slights? No. The Earth is under my protection, Loki."

Loki chuckled. "And you're doing a marvelous job with that. The humans slaughter each other in droves while you idly fret. I mean to rule them, and why should I not?"

"You think yourself above them?"

"Well, yes."

"Then you miss the truth of ruling, brother," Thor said sadly. "A throne would suit you ill."

Suddenly furious, Loki raged at Thor. "I've seen worlds you've never known about! I have grown, *Odinson,* in my exile. I have seen the true power of the Tesseract, and when I wield it—"

"Who showed you this power?" Thor interrupted. "Who controls the would-be king?"

"I am a king!" Loki screamed.

Stepping right up to his brother, Thor shouted back. "Not here! You give up the Tesseract! You give up this poisonous dream!" Then he softened. "You come home."

"I don't have it," Loki said. Furious, Thor brought Mjolnir to his hand, ready for battle. "You need the cube to send me home, but I've sent it off, I know not where."

This was a lie, Thor knew it. "You listen well, brother—"

He was cut off by Iron Man, rocketing in from the side at close to the speed of sound and hitting Thor with the force of a train.

CHAPTER 12

Tony braked and skidded to a halt as the Asgardian rolled away from him, tearing up trees and brush as he went. He got to his feet and extended a warning hand. "Do not touch me again," he said.

Tony flipped up his faceplate. "Then don't take my stuff."

"You have no idea what you're dealing with."

"Uh, Shakespeare in the Park?" Tony joked. "Doth Mother know you weareth her drapes?"

"This is beyond you, metal man," Thor said. "Loki will face Asgardian justice."

"If he gives up the cube, he's all yours. Until then..." Tony's faceplate clamped back down. "Stay out of the way."

He turned to walk back to a place where he could make a clean takeoff. "Tourist," he muttered.

That was the last straw, apparently, because the next thing Tony knew, the Asgardian's hammer had hit him about as hard as he'd ever been hit in his life. The force of the blow carried him through the trunk of a tree and laid him out flat in the dirt.

"Okay," he said. It was on.

He got up and hit the Asgardian with a repulsor blast, but that didn't keep him down for long. The Asgardian got up, raised his hammer high, and brought down a bolt of lightning, channeling it straight into Tony's suit. Inside the helmet, every heads-up display went nuts. Systems shorted out, and Tony was having a hard time moving. "Power at... four hundred percent capacity," Jarvis said calmly.

"How about that," Tony said. He took advantage of

the overcharge and unleashed another repulsor blast that drained the excess power and blew the Asgardian farther away into the forest. The Asgardian came back at him, flying through the air, and Tony flew to meet him. They swerved through the air, pounding on each other and shattering trees and rocks as they hit them. When they came back to ground, they kept grappling, exchanging punches that dented Tony's armor and caused cascading alerts through all of his systems. The Asgardian caught both of Tony's forearms. His grip was strong enough to start to crumple Tony's armor. Tony got free by firing a repulsor blast into his face, but they closed on each other again and the Asgardian nearly crushed Tony flat with a hammer blow. He jetted out of the way at the last moment and circled around for another go.

As Tony reared back for a punch and the Asgardian prepared to answer with his hammer, Captain America's shield sang out of the darkness, deflecting hard off the Asgardian's hammer and Tony's gauntlet before returning with perfect accuracy to Cap's waiting hand. They both looked up to see him standing on a nearby outcropping of rock.

"Hey!" he said, like a father showing up to break up a fight between two of his sons. "That's enough!"

He dropped down to the ground next to them. "Now I don't know what you plan on doing here—"

"I have come here to put an end to Loki's schemes," Thor said.

"Then prove it," Cap said. "Put that hammer down."

"Uh, no, bad call," Iron Man said. "He loves his hammer—"

The Asgardian interrupted Tony by smashing him out of the way with a backhand swing. "You want me to put the hammer down?" he roared, and leaped high into the air, bringing his hammer down toward Captain America.

Cap got low and held his shield up.

The impact of the hammer on the unbreakable shield sent out a shock wave that smashed every tree within a hundred yards to kindling. The Asgardian rebounded from the force of the blow, sprawling on his back. For a moment, there was silence, broken only by their heavy breathing and the sound of tree branches crashing down to earth.

Then Captain America said, "Are we done here?"

Tony powered down. As much as he hated to admit it, Cap was right. They were fighting over nothing, wasting time while their enemies got closer to using the Tesseract. Thor leaped back up the side of the mountain and picked up Loki. Tony and Cap waited while Natasha brought the Quinjet around. At least all the blown-down trees gave her an easy location to aim for.

CHAPTER 13

Bruce looked up from his work, taking a break from the delicate operation of constructing a sensor that could detect the Tesseract no matter where in the world it was being held. He looked out the window of his lab just as a squad of armed S.H.I.E.L.D. agents escorted Loki past. Loki gave Bruce a knowing smile as he went by. Bruce wasn't sure why, but he didn't like it.

He rubbed his eyes and got back to work.

Loki was sealed into a glass-walled cell, approachable only by a catwalk. At the other end of the catwalk stood Nick Fury, looking down at the control panel linked to the cell's revolving door. "In case it's unclear," Fury said, "if you try to escape, if you so much as scratch that glass..." He touched a button on the panel, and the floor below the cell opened up like an iris. Loki looked down...all the way to the ground, thousands of feet below. "Thirty thousand feet, straight down in a steel trap. You get how that works?" Riffing on what Loki had said to him before, in the lab in New Mexico, Fury pointed at Loki and said, "Ant." Then he pointed at the control panel and said, "Boot."

Loki chuckled. "It's an impressive cage," he said. "Not built, I think, for me."

"Built for something a lot stronger than you," Fury said.

"Oh, I've heard. A mindless beast. Makes play he's still a man. How desperate are you, that you call on such lost creatures to defend you?"

"How desperate am I?" Fury echoed. He walked slowly over the catwalk to stand in front of Loki. "You threaten my world with war. You steal a force you can't hope to control. You talk about peace, but you kill because it's fun. You have made me very desperate. You might not be glad that you did."

"Ooh," Loki said. "It burns you to have come so close. To have the Tesseract, to have power, unlimited power, and for what? A warm light for all mankind to share...and then to be reminded what real power is."

"Well, let me know if real power wants a magazine or something," Fury said, and walked away.

Loki knew he had been heard throughout the ship. He could hear the echoes of the speakers, and even if he had not, he always knew when people were listening to him. That was part of his power, to make them listen...and to make each of them hear something just a little different. Just what he wanted them to hear. Perhaps he was in a cage right now, but he had been in cages before. Not once had one been able to hold him for long.

"He really grows on you, doesn't he?" Bruce said. They were gathered outside the detention area to debrief and figure out what to do now that they had captured Loki. None of them believed the mission was over. It had all been a little too easy.

"Loki's going to drag this out," Cap said. "Thor, what's his play?"

"He has an army called the Chitauri," Thor said. "They're not of Asgard, nor any world known. He means to lead them against your people. They will win him the Earth, in return, I suspect, for the Tesseract."

"An army," Cap repeated. "From outer space."

"So he's building another portal," Bruce said. "That's what he needs Erik Selvig for."

"Selvig?" Thor asked.

"He's an astrophysicist," Bruce said, thinking Thor needed an explanation.

"He's a friend," Thor said.

"Loki has him under some kind of spell," Natasha said. "Along with one of ours." She didn't say who.

"I want to know why Loki let us take him," Cap said. "He's not leading an army from here."

"I don't think we should be focusing on Loki," Bruce said. "That guy's brain is a bag full of cats. You can smell the crazy on him."

Thor took a step toward Bruce. "Have a care how you speak," he warned. "Loki is beyond reason, but he is of Asgard . . . and he is my brother."

"He killed eighty people in two days," Natasha pointed out.

Acknowledging this, Thor backed down a little. "He's adopted."

Bruce was already moving on to the problem at hand. "I think it's about the mechanics," he said. "Iridium. What do they need the iridium for?" They knew Barton had stolen a supply of iridium from under the Stuttgart Museum, taking advantage of Loki's diversion. But they didn't yet know what Selvig could use it for.

"It's a stabilizing agent," Tony Stark said as he

entered with Coulson. "It means the portal won't col-lapse on itself like it did at S.H.I.E.L.D." Thor had turned to meet Tony as he came in. The Asgardian's posture was aggressive, to say the least. "No hard feelings, Point Break," Tony said. "You've got a mean swing."

Thor didn't understand the joke, but he under-stood the point of what Tony was saying. He let it go. It wasn't the first time he had fought with someone who turned out to be an ally.

Tony went on. "Also, iridium will mean the portal can open as wide and stay open as long as Loki wants." He had wandered out into Fury's command station, and now he put a hand over one eye and tried to watch all of the monitors. "How does Fury even see these?"

"He turns," Maria Hill said. Clearly she didn't think it was funny.

"Sounds exhausting," Tony said. "Anyway, the rest of the raw materials Agent Barton can get his hands on pretty easily. The only major component he still needs is a power source with high energy density. Something to kick-start the cube."

"When did you become an expert in thermonuclear astrophysics?" Hill asked. She was still irritated by his mocking of Nick Fury.

Without missing a beat, Tony said, "Last night. Selvig's notes. The extraction theory papers. Am I the only one who did the reading?"

"Does Loki need any particular kind of power source?" Cap asked. Like the rest of them, he was learning to ignore Tony's constant joking.

"He'd have to heat the cube to a hundred and twenty million Kelvin just to break through the Coulomb barrier," Bruce said. He was talking about the physical barriers to creating a portal between different places in space and time.

"Unless Selvig has figured out how to stabilize the quantum tunneling effect," Tony said.

Bruce shrugged. "Well, if he could do that, he could achieve heavy ion fusion at any reactor on the planet."

"Finally, someone who speaks English," Tony said.

Cap looked at Thor. "Is that what just happened?"

Tony reached out to shake Bruce's hand. "It's good to finally meet you, Dr. Banner. Your work in anti-electron collisions is unparalleled. And I'm a huge fan of the way you lose control and turn into an enormous green rage monster."

"Thanks," Bruce said. He didn't look too excited about Tony mentioning the Hulk.

"Dr. Banner is only here to track the cube," Fury said as he came in. "I was hoping you might join him."

"Let's start with that stick of his," Cap said. "It may be magical, but it works an awful lot like a Hydra weapon." He'd seen plenty of those in action when he was fighting the Red Skull in Europe. Loki's scepter seemed to use the same kind of energy, or at least that's what it looked like to him.

"I don't know about that, but it is powered by the cube," Fury said. "And I would like to know how Loki used it to turn two of the sharpest men I know into his personal flying monkeys."

"Monkeys?" Thor asked. "I do not understand."

"I do!" Steve said. "I understood that reference!"

It was a small victory for him. Most of his slang was seventy years out of date.

"Shall we play, Doctor?" Tony asked Bruce.

Bruce gestured toward the corridor that led to his lab. The scepter was there and so was all of their equipment. "This way, sir."

CHAPTER 14

O nce they arrived in the lab, Bruce got straight to work while Tony looked over the equipment. The doctor scanned a device over Loki's scepter. "The gamma rays are definitely consistent with Selvig's reports on the Tesseract. But it's going to take weeks to process."

Tony was already looking at the structure of the S.H.I.E.L.D. computers they had available. "If we bypass their mainframe and route directly to the

Homer cluster, we can clock this at around six hundred teraflops," he said. That was a lot faster than what Fury was working with as the system stood.

"All I packed was a toothbrush," Bruce chuckled.

"You know, you should come by Stark Tower sometime. Top ten floors, all R & D," Tony said. "You'd love it."

"Thanks, but the last time I was in New York, I kind of...broke Harlem."

"Well, I promise a stress-free environment. No tension, no surprises..." As he spoke, Tony walked behind Bruce and gave him a little zap with an electrical instrument.

"Ow!" Bruce said.

Tony looked closely at him. "Nothing?" He'd been testing Bruce to see how well he controlled the Hulk. The little shock hadn't provoked any kind of unusual reaction, which Tony seemed to find a little disappointing.

"Are you nuts?" said Captain America as he came into the lab.

"Jury's out," Tony said. Turning back to Bruce, he

asked, "You really have got a lid on it, haven't you? What's your secret? Mellow jazz, bongo drums...?"

"Is everything a joke to you?" Cap said.

"Funny things are," Tony said.

"Threatening the safety of everyone on this ship isn't funny. No offense, Doc."

"It's all right. I wouldn't have come on board if I couldn't handle pointy things and little surprises."

Tony shook his head. "You're tiptoeing, big man. You need to strut."

"And you need to focus on the problem, Mr. Stark," Captain America said. What was Tony doing, trying to get Bruce to turn into the Hulk? What good would that do any of them? They had more important things to do than stand around while Tony Stark played stupid games.

"Do you think I'm not?" Tony asked him. He paused and then fired off a series of questions. "Why did Fury call us in? Why now? Why not before? What isn't he telling us? I can't do the equation unless I have all the variables."

Cap wasn't following his line of thinking. None of that mattered to him. "You think Fury's hiding something?"

"He's a spy. Captain, he's *the* spy. His secrets have secrets." Tony waved at Bruce, who was buried in his instruments. "It's bugging him, too. Isn't it?"

"Ahh, I just want to finish my work here," Bruce said, trying to stay out of it.

"Doctor," Cap said. He wasn't going to let this go.

Bruce sighed and took off his glasses. "'A warm light for all mankind,'" he quoted. "Loki's jab at Fury about the cube."

"I heard it," Cap said.

"I think that was meant for you," Bruce said to Tony. "Even if Barton didn't tell Loki about the tower, it was still all over the news."

"The Stark Tower? That big ugly..." Tony looked up. "Building?" Cap finished. "In New York?"

"It's powered by an Arc Reactor, a self-sustaining energy source," Bruce pointed out. "That building will run itself for, what? A year?"

"That's just the prototype," Tony said. "I'm kind of the only name in clean energy right now," he explained to Cap. "That's what he's getting at."

Cap didn't know what he meant by "clean energy," but he could tell it was another of Tony's typical boasts, so he let it pass.

"So why didn't S.H.I.E.L.D. bring him in on the Tesseract project?" Bruce asked. "What are they doing in the energy business in the first place?"

"I should probably look into that once my decryption program finishes breaking into all of S.H.I.E.L.D.'s secure files." Tony looked at a tiny computer tablet, barely bigger than a credit card.

"I'm sorry," Cap said. "Did you say—"

"Jarvis has been running it since I hit the bridge," Tony said. "In a few hours, I'll know every dirty secret S.H.I.E.L.D. has ever tried to hide."

"Yet you're confused about why they didn't want you around," Cap said.

"An intelligence organization that fears intelligence?" Tony said. "That's historically . . . not awesome."

Cap felt his temper starting to rise. He got it under

control. There was one angle on their situation that none of them had talked about yet. "I think Loki's trying to wind us up," he said. "This is a man who means to start a war, and if we don't stay focused, he'll succeed. We have orders. We should follow them."

"Following's not really my style," Tony said through a mouthful of dried blueberries.

"And you're all about style, aren't you?" Cap said.

"Steve," Bruce said, "tell me none of this smells a little funky to you."

Cap looked back and forth between the two scientists. Bruce could tell he was struggling with something...but he also wasn't going to share it. He was too much of a good soldier for that.

"Just find the cube," he said, and walked out of the lab.

"That's the guy my dad never shut up about?" Tony said when he was gone. "Maybe they should have kept him on ice."

"He's not wrong about Loki." Bruce was adding new data to a screen showing surveillance results. "He does have the jump on us."

"What he's got is an Acme dynamite kit," Tony said. "It's going to blow up in his face...and I'm going to be there when it does."

"Yeah. I'll read all about it."

"Or you'll be suiting up with the rest of us."

Bruce shook his head with a regretful smile. "No, see, I don't get a suit of armor. I'm exposed. Like a nerve. It's a nightmare."

Tony stood on the other side of the transparent screen Bruce was using. "You know," he said, "I've got a cluster of shrapnel trying every second to crawl its way into my heart." He tapped the miniature Arc Reactor in his chest. "This stops it. This little circle of light, it's part of me now. Not just armor. It's a... terrible privilege."

"But you can control it," Bruce said. He was willing to listen to Tony, but he didn't feel like being lectured on what it was like to have problems. Bruce Banner knew about problems.

"Because I learned how," Tony said.

Bruce shook his head. "It's different."

"Hey." Suddenly serious, Tony swiped all the data

away from the screen so they could see each other clearly. "I read all about your accident. That much gamma exposure should have killed you."

"So you're staying that the Hulk...the other guy...saved my life? That's nice," Bruce said. "Nice sentiment. Saved it for what?"

"I guess we'll find out," Tony said.

Bruce swiped the data back onto the screen. "You may not enjoy that."

Tony also got back to work. "And you just might."

CHAPTER 15

Thor watched over Coulson's shoulder as the agent showed him S.H.I.E.L.D.'s current files on Jane Foster. When he had learned that Loki had captured Erik Selvig, his first thought had been of Jane. Thor had destroyed the Bifrost to save the Nine Realms, but he had also cut himself off from her...or so he had thought. It was a terrible decision to make, sacrificing love for duty—yet Thor had done it. If necessary, he would do it again. He hoped it would not be necessary, though, and that was one reason why he had asked Coulson about Jane.

"As soon as Loki took Dr. Selvig, we moved Jane Foster," Coulson explained to Thor. "They've got an excellent observatory in Tromsø. She was asked to consult there . . . very suddenly . . . yesterday. Handsome fee, private plane, very remote. She'll be safe."

"Thank you," Thor said. "It's no accident, Loki taking Erik Selvig. I dread what he plans for Erik once he's done. Erik is a good man."

"He talks about you a lot," Coulson said. "You changed his life. You changed everything around here."

Thor shook his head. At times like this, he wished no Asgardian had even come to Midgard—or, as the people here called it, Earth. "They were better as they were," he said, meaning Selvig and Jane Foster. "We pretend on Asgard that we're more advanced, but we come here battling like bilgesnipe."

"What?"

"Bilgesnipe," Thor repeated. "You know. Huge, scaly, big antlers." He mimed the antlers with his fingers. "You don't have those?"

"I don't think so," Coulson said.

"Well. They are repulsive, and they trample everything in their path." Thor looked out into the sky, gathering his thoughts. "When I first came to Earth," he went on, "Loki's rage followed me here, and your people paid the price. Now, again. In my youth, I courted war."

"War hasn't started yet," Fury said from nearby at his command platform. "You think you could make Loki tell us where the Tesseract is?"

This possibility hadn't occurred to Thor. "I do not know," he said. "Loki's mind is far afield. It's not just power he craves. It's vengeance, upon me. There's no pain that would pry that need from him."

"A lot of guys think that, until the pain starts," Fury said.

Thor held Fury's gaze. It was not the first time he had looked at a one-eyed man who posed him a difficult question. "What are you asking me to do?" he asked, wanting Fury to be clear and to own his words.

"I'm asking what you are prepared to do," Fury said quietly.

"Loki is a prisoner," Thor said. He thought Fury was testing him, seeing if he would violate his ideals to find out something they all needed to know. But Thor would not.

"Then why do I feel like he's the only person on this boat who wants to be here?" Fury asked. Thor had no answer.

Loki paced in his cell and became conscious that someone was near. He turned and saw the woman they called the Black Widow standing on the catwalk. "There's not many people who can sneak up on me," he said.

"But you figured I'd come," she said.

"After," Loki said. "After whatever tortures Fury can concoct, you would appear as a friend, as a balm. And I would cooperate." It was a typical approach. Cause misery, and then let someone appear as a friendly face. The miserable person would say anything to keep this friend. Loki had seen strong men break this way, many times.

Yet this did not appear to be what he had expected. No one had questioned him. No one had caused him any discomfort at all, save the embarrassment of being imprisoned in this cell.

"I want to know what you've done to Agent Barton," she said.

"I would say I've expanded his mind."

"And once you've won, once you're king of the mountain, what happens to his mind?" she asked.

Loki started to think he had more control over this situation than he had known. "Is this love, Agent Romanoff?" he asked, needling her a little.

"Love is for children," she said. "I owe him a debt."

He came closer to the glass. "Tell me."

"Before I worked for S.H.I.E.L.D., I . . . well, I made

a name for myself," she said. "I have a very specific skill set. I didn't care who I used it for. Or on. I got on S.H.I.E.L.D.'s radar in a bad way. Agent Barton was sent to take me out. He made a different call."

An interesting story, Loki thought. She has much to atone for. He could hear some of her memories, from before her first encounter with Barton. *Little girl,* he thought, *you've done some very bad things. And now you think you owe Clint Barton your life...but there is more to it.* Loki could tell there was something in her mind that he was not quite uncovering. He pushed a little more. "And what will you do if I vow to spare him?"

"Not let you out," she said.

He grinned. "No, but I like this. Your world in the balance, and you bargain for one man."

"Regimes fall every day. I tend not to weep over that," she said. "I'm Russian. Or I was."

"And what are you now?"

She dodged the question, but again Loki had the sense he had come close to understanding something important about her. "It's really not that complicated," she said. "I got red in my ledger, I'd like to wipe it out."

Red in my ledger. She spoke of life debts as if they were lines in an accountant's records, black ink for profit and red ink for debt. Loki understood now... and he pounced.

"Can you?" he asked. "Can you wipe out that much red?" He listed for her some of the things he knew she had done. "Dreykov's daughter... São Paulo... the hospital fire? Barton told me everything." This was a lie. Barton had told Loki certain things about Romanoff, but he was also guessing some others. He pushed ahead. Now that he understood her, he could break her. "Your ledger is dripping, it's gushing red, and you think saving a man no more virtuous than yourself will change anything? Pathetic. You lie and kill in the service of liars and killers. You pretend to be separate, to have your own code, something that makes up for the horrors, but they are part of you and they will never go away."

He had done it. The Black Widow was weeping, and she turned away. "You monster."

"Oh, no," Loki said, loving every moment of this. "You brought the monster."

Then she turned around and her face was completely devoid of emotion again. "So," she said briskly. "Banner. That's your play."

"What?" Loki couldn't understand how she had gathered her composure so quickly—and then he did understand. She was a superb actress! Or not even an actress, for he could see through a conscious performance. She was something else. She had been broken down and remade so many times, with so many identities, that she could put them on and take them off at will. And Loki had gotten lost in those emotional costume changes.

He had been outwitted by a mortal. Unthinkable.

She spun and started walking fast, talking into her mic as she went. "Loki means to unleash the Hulk. Keep Banner in the lab. I'm on my way. Send Thor as well."

When she had gotten to the elevator, she turned. With infuriating courtesy, she said to Loki, "Thank you for your cooperation."

Loki watched the elevator door close. He was astonished, and furious…and also, he had to admit, a little impressed. Not many people could beat Loki at his own game. But one of them, at least this time, was Natasha Romanoff.

CHAPTER 16

Nick Fury came into the lab with a look on his face that said it wasn't just a social call. He singled Tony out right away. "What are you doing, Mr. Stark?"

So S.H.I.E.L.D. cybersecurity had finally noticed Jarvis's infiltration. "Uh, kind of been wondering the same thing about you," Tony answered. He didn't look upset that Fury had found him out. Instead he looked ready for a confrontation. They needed answers.

"You're supposed to be locating the Tesseract," Fury reminded them.

"We are," Bruce said. He pointed at a screen running his search algorithm using all of the spectrometers S.H.I.E.L.D. had been able to commandeer. "The model's locked, and we're sweeping for the signature now. When we get a hit, we'll have the location within half a mile."

"Yeah, then you get the cube back. No muss, no fuss." Tony kept going and changed the subject. "What is Phase Two?"

Something banged on a table near the lab door, and they all turned to see that Captain America had entered and set down a prototype rifle of some kind, loud enough to purposely draw their attention.

No, Tony realized when he'd gotten a closer look at the rifle. Not a prototype. An old weapon. A Hydra weapon from World War II.

"Phase Two is S.H.I.E.L.D. uses the cube to make weapons," Cap said. "Sorry," he added to Tony. "Computer was moving a little slow for me." He'd been worried by what Tony and Bruce had said. He wasn't going to tell them that, but it was true. When he'd left the lab, he'd headed for an archive level deep down inside the Helicarrier. It was a hangar space filled with steel crates, extending many levels above and below him....

And in some of those crates, he had found a lot of weapons like the one he was now showing the rest of the team.

Fury saw that he couldn't duck their questions anymore. He started trying to explain. "Rogers, we gathered everything related to the Tesseract," Fury said. "This does not mean that we're making—"

"I'm sorry, Nick," Tony interrupted. He spun a display around so it showed classified S.H.I.E.L.D. designs for Tesseract-powered weaponry. "Why were you lying?"

"I was wrong, Director," Cap said. "The world hasn't changed a bit." He looked angry and disappointed. Captain America was a big believer in shooting straight and telling the truth. He didn't like spies and he didn't like lies, and now he saw he was knee-deep in both.

"Did you know about this?" Bruce asked Natasha as she came in with Thor.

She glanced at Fury and then said calmly, "You want to think about removing yourself from this environment, Doctor."

"I was in Calcutta," Bruce said. "I was pretty well removed."

"Loki is manipulating you," she said.

"And you've been doing what, exactly?"

Natasha gave him an are-you-serious? look. "You didn't come here because I batted my eyelashes at you."

"Yes, and I'm not leaving because suddenly you get a little twitchy," Bruce said. He kept his calm, but they could all tell he wasn't happy. None of them wanted him to get upset; they'd all seen the video of what happened the last time the Hulk went on a rampage. "I'd like to know why S.H.I.E.L.D. is using the Tesseract to build weapons of mass destruction," Bruce finished.

"Because of him," Fury said, pointing at Thor.

"Me?"

"Last year, Earth had a visitor from another planet who had a grudge match that leveled a small town,"

Fury said. "We learned that not only are we not alone, but we are hopelessly, hilariously, outgunned."

"My people want nothing but peace with your planet," Thor said.

"But you're not the only people out there, are you? And you're not the only threat." Fury looked at each of them in turn, letting them know he was talking about them. "The world's filling up with people who can't be matched, can't be controlled."

"Like you controlled the cube?" Cap shot back.

"Your work with the Tesseract is what drew Loki to it, and his allies," Thor said. "It is a signal to all the realms that the Earth is ready for a higher form of war."

"A higher form? You forced our hand," Fury argued. "We had to come up with something."

"A nuclear deterrent," Tony said. "Because that always calms everything right down."

"Remind me again how you made your fortune, Stark," Fury said coldly.

"I'm sure if he still made weapons, Stark would be neck-deep," Cap said.

Tony held up one hand. "Hold on. How is this now about me?"

"I'm sorry," Cap said. "Isn't everything?" He and Tony faced each other, looking like they were ready to fight.

"I thought humans were more evolved than this," Thor commented.

Tony turned on Thor. "Excuse me, did we come to your planet and blow stuff up?"

Just like that, all of them were arguing. Cap and Tony were nose to nose, while Bruce and Natasha fired remarks back and forth. Thor stood off to the side, contempt plain on his face.

None of them noticed when the gem set into Loki's scepter started to glow.

CHAPTER 17

Tony and Cap squared off over an argument that they couldn't even remember starting. Tony was still mad about the last thing Cap had said to him...whatever it was. He gave Cap a little brushback with his shoulder. "Back off," Cap said.

"I'm starting to want you to make me," Tony said.

Cap stood his ground. "Big man in a suit of armor. Take that off, what are you?"

Tony had an answer ready for this one. "Genius, billionaire, playboy, philanthropist."

"I know guys with none of that worth ten of you," Cap said. "I've seen the footage. The only thing you really fight for is yourself. You're not the guy to make the sacrifice play, to lay down on a wire and let the other guy crawl over you."

Tony smirked. "I think I would just cut the wire."

"Always a way out. You know, you may not be a threat, but you better stop pretending to be a hero."

"A hero? Like you? You're a lab experiment, Rogers. Everything special about you came out of a bottle."

"Put on the suit," Cap said. "Let's go a few rounds."

Thor laughed. "You people are so petty...and tiny."

"Yeah, this is a team," Bruce said.

Fury could see things were spiraling out of control. He started trying to get them all back on track. "Agent Romanoff," he said, "would you escort Dr. Banner back to—"

"Where?" Bruce interrupted. "My room? You rented my room."

Nobody had said it out loud, but they all knew the cell currently holding Loki was designed for the Hulk. Fury admitted it. "The cell was just in case—"

Again Bruce interrupted. "You needed to kill me." The words hung there. Nobody contradicted him. "But you can't. I know. I tried." Bruce swallowed. It was hard for him to admit that. "So I moved on. I focused on helping people. I was good. Until you dragged me into this freak show and put everyone else in danger. You want to know my secret, Agent Romanoff? You want to know how I stay calm?"

"Dr. Banner," Cap said. "Put down the scepter."

Bruce looked down. He hadn't even known he'd picked it up. He looked back up and saw Natasha's hand on her sidearm. Fury was also ready to draw. The others were drawing back from him as well.

Even though he could see what was going on, the hostility in the air was still thick enough that Bruce didn't know whether he could back everyone down . . . or whether he could back himself down. He could feel tension rising inside him. He could feel the monster trying to get loose.

Luckily for all of them, that was when the computer beeped. 95% MATCH glowed a red status message on the screen. "Sorry, kids, you don't get to see my party trick after all," Bruce said. He set the scepter down and went to see where the Tesseract was. That was the only thing that could have set off that particular alert.

But even though he was now refocused on the mission, the others still bickered. Loki had gotten into their heads, sowing discord and setting them against each other.

"The Tesseract belongs to Asgard," Thor said. "No human—"

"I'll go after it," Tony said.

"No you don't," Cap said, stepping into his way. He wasn't ready to forget the way Tony had insulted him.

Tony stopped just short of making physical contact with Cap. "You going to stop me?"

"Put on the suit," Cap said, deadly serious.

Fury didn't know how it had happened, but they were at each other's throats, again, or still...except

Bruce, who was absorbed in the data coming from the gamma radiation scanning program. 100% MATCH said the red status bar.

"Oh no," Bruce said, and that's when the first of the explosions rocked the Helicarrier.

CHAPTER 18

Clint Barton and Loki's hand-picked strike team were in a stolen Quinjet with a faked S.H.I.E.L.D. call sign, 26-Bravo. That got them close enough that by the time the air-traffic officer on the Helicarrier knew something was wrong, it was already too late.

Barton's first shot hit the Helicarrier's hull in front of one of the giant turbines that kept it in the air. It was just a beacon, meant to guide in the stealth missiles to follow. They would disable the Helicarrier, and while S.H.I.E.L.D. scrambled to react, he would be in and out with what he wanted.

When the explosions went off, he immediately heard Hill and Fury yelling over the Helicarrier comm system. He and Loki's tech team had hacked the Helicarrier's frequency as soon as they were within range. "Hill!" Fury called.

"External detonation. Number Three engine is down," Hill answered.

Sure was, Barton thought. He was watching pieces of it fall, trailing smoke and fire on their way to the ground.

"Somebody's got to get outside and patch that engine," she went on.

Barton frowned.

"I'm on it," he heard Tony Stark say. "Engine Three. I'll meet you there." He was talking to another member of Fury's team, but Barton didn't know who. It wouldn't matter. He would make sure they didn't get there...or if they did, it wouldn't make any difference.

The Quinjet hovered at the infiltration point, an external hatch chosen to give them quick access to the detention area. That was where Loki would be. His team made entry, nice and clean. "Keep that engine down!" he ordered the fire team. Then he headed off himself to spring Loki. Dr. Selvig had the machine almost ready. It was go time.

The explosions that had taken out the Number Three engine also collapsed several of the Helicarrier's interior decks—including part of Bruce's lab. Natasha and Bruce lay pinned under steel beams and other wreckage down in a maintenance area. She was lying on a steel grate floor. Bruce was near her. "Romanoff?" came Fury's voice through her comm.

"We're okay," she said, even though she couldn't get herself loose. Her leg was caught under an angled beam that jammed into the corner where the floor met the wall.

She looked over at Bruce. He was facedown a few

feet away, fists clenched, making a constricted groaning noise. His legs were hidden by debris that pinned him in place. Natasha got uneasy. She didn't like the noises he was making. "We're okay, right?"

He kept groaning. The sounds got more and more intense...and less and less human.

"Bruce? You've got to fight it. This is just what Loki wants. Are you okay? Are you hurt?" Two techs came running to help them, and she waved them away quickly. She didn't want them around if Bruce lost control of the Hulk. "We're going to be okay," she repeated. "All right? I swear on my life I will get you out of this, you will walk away and never—"

"Your life?!" he roared, looking up at her. His face terrified her. She could see the green gamma radiance in his eyes, and the rage in his expression was like nothing she had ever seen on a human face. He had lost control.

"Bruce?" she said again. But it was too late. She saw the transformation begin.

He fell and rolled, his body heaving. His skin began to turn green, and huge layers of muscle expanded with a crackling sound as his bones and joints also grew with incredible speed. His roars grew louder, monstrous, rattling the wreckage around them. Natasha knew she had to get out of there. As the Hulk, he wouldn't recognize her. The only person he'd ever recognized was Betty Ross, and she wasn't around at the moment. Natasha wouldn't stand a chance.

With a last heave and twist, she freed herself from the fallen beam and ran. At that moment, the Hulk turned and saw her. She vaulted up a stairway and onto the next level. The Hulk swiped at the stairway and shredded it into scrap metal. Loki had gotten what he wanted. He must have been trying to time it so he could manipulate Bruce into becoming the Hulk right as his soldiers came to attack the Helicarrier. The Hulk would do at least as much damage from the inside as the rogue Quinjet could do from the outside.

Natasha kept running, and the Hulk came right behind her. For a moment, she thought she'd lost him, but then he came at her out of the shadows, roaring.

He was like walking rage, a single-minded engine of destruction. She shot a hole in the pipe over his head. Steam shot out of it into the Hulk's eyes, stopping him for just the moment she needed to get a head start. She ran as fast as she could, but she knew she wasn't going to stay away from him for long. He came after her, smashing through bulkheads and doorways like they weren't even there and roaring the whole time.

She ducked to one side, and he shot past her, slamming into the opposite wall of a garage area. The Hulk looked around. He saw her.

This is it, Natasha thought.

At that moment, something exploded through the wall and into the Hulk. Natasha caught a glimpse of blond hair and armor before both Thor and the Hulk crashed through the opposite wall and into one of the main hangar decks. Flight crews and support staff scattered.

Natasha scrambled to her feet. Thor had saved her life. At least for the moment.

CHAPTER 19

B ring us around heading one eight zero!" Fury ordered. "We need to get over the water!" He couldn't have the Helicarrier coming down over a populated area. Civilian casualties would be in the thousands.

"Navigation systems are still recalibrating after the explosion," an officer said. "We—"

Fury pinned the officer with a one-eyed glare. "Is the sun coming up?"

"Yes…"

"Then put it on the left!" he snapped, furious that his navigators couldn't get their heads out of the machines long enough to figure out that if the sun was in the east, that made it simple to figure out which way was south. "Get us over water! One more turbine goes down, and we drop."

The Helicarrier heeled around and accelerated south, as smoke poured from the shattered turbine housing. Over the intercoms, Fury heard gunshots. Loki's team almost certainly led by Clint Barton had boarded the Helicarrier looking for their Asgardian leader.

Steve got to the edge of the turbine mount about the same time as Tony. "I'm here!" he called out.

"Good," Tony said, dropping into view and hovering in the Iron Man armor to survey the wreckage. He had the suit on, and Steve could hear his voice through the earbud microphone all S.H.I.E.L.D.

personnel wore. At least that channel was still intact; if they lost communications, they'd be done for.

The hole torn out of the Helicarrier was huge, seemingly fatal, but they were keeping it in the air. Fury's staff said the turbine was just jammed and might hold together if they could get it started again. Most of the damage was to the structure holding it...and to the areas just inside the hull, including Bruce's lab.

"Let's see what we've got," Tony said. He started muttering to himself, then called out to Steve. "I need you to get to that engine control panel and tell me which relays are in overload position."

Steve jumped and swung across the thirty-thousand-foot drop, getting to the other side of the hole in the Helicarrier's hull and pulling open the panel Tony had pointed at. He saw a lot of circuits. "What's it look like in there?" Tony asked.

"It seems to run on some form of electricity," Steve said.

Tony was shoving loose huge pieces of debris that

prevented the turbine blades from rotating. "Well, you're not wrong," he said.

Steve fumed. He wasn't here for technical support. But that was all he could do at the moment. He had to swallow his pride and do what Tony asked or they were all going to go down in flames. Literally. He looked at the panel and saw that none of the connections had shorted out.

"Okay," Steve said, "the relays are intact. What's our next move?"

Tony stood inside the turbine housing, looking at the blades. He'd cleared most of the debris jamming the rotors. "Even if I clear the rotors," he said, "this thing won't reengage without a jump. I'm going to have to get in there and push."

"If that thing gets up to speed, you'll get shredded," Steve said.

"See that red lever?" Tony pointed at a control panel across a shattered part of the floor. Steve jumped and landed near it. "It'll slow the blades down enough for me to get out. Stand by it and wait for my word."

The Hulk stomped around the flight deck, roaring. He saw Thor and swung a fist twice the size of Thor's head. Thor caught it in both hands, straining to hold both the Hulk's arm and his attention. "We are not your enemies, Banner," he grunted. "Try to think!"

In answer, the Hulk punched him through the wall.

Thor got up and watched the Hulk coming after him. Now this was a fight! He held out a hand, waiting for Mjolnir to return to him. Mjolnir smashed through another wall and reached Thor's hand just as the charging Hulk came within striking distance.

Thor met the Hulk with a blow from Mjolnir that rattled his teeth. The Hulk flew backward into a jet plane, caving in its fuselage and tearing off part of its tail. Enraged, he threw part of the plane at Thor, who ducked and hurled Mjolnir at him again.

The Hulk caught the hammer, and a fierce grin spread over his face…then he toppled backward and Mjolnir pinned him to the floor of the hangar.

None but I can lift Mjolnir, Thor thought. *Not even this giant.*

The plates of the floor buckled under the Hulk as he strained to get Mjolnir off the ground. Thor seized the opportunity—to seize Mjolnir! Then he jumped on the Hulk's back, using Mjolnir's handle to try to choke the Hulk into submission. He hoped that if the Hulk fell unconscious, Bruce would return.

Yet even his Asgardian strength was not enough to bring the Hulk down immediately. The great green creature thrashed around the hangar, destroying aircraft and machinery. Thor hung on grimly, knowing that at least he was keeping the Hulk's attention away from those who would suffer much more than he would.

Maria Hill saw the battle between Thor and the Hulk via surveillance cameras. Everyone was occupied keeping the Helicarrier in the air and looking for the team that had boarded from the stolen Quinjet.

"We need a complete evac of the lower hangar level," she said, and left the bridge to oversee it herself.

A clinking sound drew her attention downward...to see a concussion grenade rolling across the floor. "Grenade!" she shouted. A moment later, it went off.

The bridge was suddenly full of hostile soldiers. Hill and Fury were in the fight of their lives. Gunfire echoed throughout the bridge. Stray bullets cracked the heavy glass windows and chewed computer terminals apart in showers of sparks. Hill and Fury returned fire, trying to keep the attackers away from the command consoles. The evacuation of the lower hangar decks would have to take care of itself, Hill thought. A bullet ricocheted near her and a fragment of it cut her cheek. She had more pressing problems.

Downstairs, Coulson heard the alarm. *Perimeter breach. Attackers are wearing S.H.I.E.L.D. gear.* He got to a secret locker and pressed his thumb against the security pad. Before it could open, the Hulk and Thor exploded up through the floor, tearing the security features apart.

So much for containment, Coulson thought.

"We have the Hulk and Thor on Level Four," he said. "Levels Two and Three are dark."

Maria Hill knew that if something didn't distract the Hulk, he would tear the Helicarrier apart...which was, of course, exactly what Loki wanted. "Escort six-oh," she said. "Engage the big man. Get his attention. Don't get too close."

"Copy that," came the pilot's voice.

The S.H.I.E.L.D. escort fighter brought itself around to the location Hill specified. She heard the pilot say *"Target acquired."* Glancing over at the instrument console on the bridge, she saw one of the monitors giving a feed from the escort. The Hulk was slamming Thor around like a rag doll.

"Target engaged," the pilot said, and fired a long burst from a 20-millimeter rapid-fire cannon.

It got the Hulk's attention, all right. Hill fired at one of the invading soldiers, dropping him, then looked back to see the Hulk, in a berserk fury, jumping out of the Helicarrier toward the jet! *"Target angry! Target angry!"* shouted the pilot.

The Hulk landed on the plane just behind the cockpit and started tearing pieces from its fuselage. *"Mayday, Mayday,"* the pilot called. He ejected, his parachute blooming in the sky below the Helicarrier.

The Hulk, and the wreckage of the plane, fell away toward the ground and disappeared.

CHAPTER 20

Tony was almost done cutting through the rest of the debris blocking the turbine funnel. He had built a ruby-laser torch into the Iron Man suit for just such an occasion...or, you know, a similar one. When he thought he'd cut enough, he kicked the pieces of debris several times until they fell away. *There we go,* he thought. Should be able to get the turbine going again now.

He glanced over as sparks caught his eye. They were

caused by ricocheting bullets. The bad guys were after Captain America. So far he was holding his position next to the red lever. That's what Tony needed him to do...but he would only be able to do it for so long if Loki's fighters got a clear shot at him.

On the bridge, Fury and Hill and their surviving support personnel were holding off Loki's men...but they were also trapped. Fury needed to figure out a way to break them loose before Barton found a way to Loki.

And speaking of Barton, there he was! But Fury didn't see him before he had already fired an arrow. Fury gasped, anticipating the impact on his body— but Barton hadn't fired at him. He was aiming at the command console. His arrow didn't have a point but a grouping of pins. They hit a pin jack on the console and immediately the entire instrument panel flashed MALFUNCTION and began to power down.

Fury also heard one of the remaining turbines

powering down. If he couldn't do something about that soon, they were all going to be dead.

He fired at Barton, who didn't stick around to engage him.

"We are in an uncontrolled descent," a voice over the speakers said. The Helicarrier tipped steeply enough that some of the fighter aircraft spilled off its flight deck.

"It's Barton," Fury said over the speakers. "He's headed for the detention level."

He put it out over the speakers because he wanted Natasha Romanoff to hear.

She did. "This is Agent Romanoff," she said. "I copy."

We might get out of this after all, thought Nick Fury.

Tony powered up his boot thrusters all the way and started leaning into the closest turbine blade. He had to get them up to a speed at which they would be self-sustaining—but not much faster than that or he wouldn't have a chance to get out before the spinning blades mulched him. The first few revolutions were slow, as the blade tips scoured away bent and torn bits of metal from the inside of the turbine housing—but once those got smoothed out, things went better. Pretty soon Tony was going to have the whole thing up to speed.

Which apparently was just in time, he thought. He could feel the Helicarrier lurching around him and Jarvis had mentioned that another of the turbines was powering down.

He held the Helicarrier up all by himself, more or less, or at least slowed its rate of descent, trying to get this engine back online so he could rejoin the fight and try to keep the rest of the team alive.

With the Hulk out of the way—though, Thor hoped, not hurt—Thor could get back to his real task, which was making sure Loki did not escape. He charged into the detention level and saw Loki just getting out through the glass revolving door that held him! Thor ran, arms spread wide to tackle Loki back into the cell.

But as he made contact with his brother, the illusion vanished! Thor skidded on his stomach into the cell, as the door closed behind him. He spun and got up to see Loki there, gloating on the catwalk. "Are you ever not going to fall for that?" he smirked.

Thor roared and pounded Mjolnir into the cell wall. The glass cracked but held. Loki looked nervous, but when he saw Thor couldn't get out, his face broke into a relieved smile. So did the guard with him. "The humans think us immortal. Should we test that?"

He went to the control panel that could drop the cell out the bottom of the Helicarrier.

There was a small noise, and the guard dropped silently to the floor. Thor turned in the direction of the sound and saw Agent Coulson, holding a very large gun. "Move away, please," he said.

Loki did, watching Coulson warily.

"You like this?" Coulson asked, meaning the gun. "We started working on the prototype after you sent the Destroyer. Even I don't know what it does." He powered it up, and rings along its barrel glowed bright orange. "Want to find out?"

But Loki wasn't there in front of him. Thor saw it too late to do anything. That Loki was an illusion... and the real Loki was behind Coulson.

He stabbed Coulson in the back with his scepter and watched as the brave agent sank to the floor. "No!" Thor cried out. He pounded the cell wall but could not damage it further.

Without a word, Loki walked slowly back to the control panel. Coulson watched him go. He couldn't get up. Thor could see he was badly wounded.

Loki tapped the touch screen, and the floor disappeared. Air roared up into the Helicarrier from the opening. Then Loki touched another control, and Thor dropped through the Helicarrier's lower levels and out into empty air, falling thousands of feet toward the ground.

CHAPTER 21

Natasha found Barton near Loki's cell. She almost got the drop on him but something—she would never know what—clued him in to her presence and he spun at the last moment, letting fly an arrow that came so close she felt the whisper of its passage. Then she closed in on him and they fought hand to hand. Barton was very good, but Natasha was among the best who had ever lived. Barton had the upper hand at first because he was skilled at using his bow as a weapon. Natasha caught hold of it and got it away from him, thinking now she had the advantage, but he pulled a knife and once again she was fighting for her life. She couldn't believe it. She was closer to him than anyone, but he was coming after her like she was just another target.

She concentrated on keeping the knife away from her, but they were fighting on a narrow catwalk. Once Barton got close, his superior strength came into play. She locked both her hands around his right wrist, holding the knife away from her, but it got closer and closer....

Desperate, Natasha bit him on the arm. Barton shouted out in surprise, and she used the momentary distraction to swing him around and smash his head into one of the steel posts supporting the catwalk.

He went down and stayed down for a few moments. Then he looked up at her and said, "Natasha?"

But she wasn't ready to believe he had freed himself from Loki's spell. Not just yet. Natasha stepped in and knocked Barton unconscious with one final punch.

Loki watched on a monitor screen as the prison cell fell...and fell...and smashed into the earth near the ocean far below, shattering into thousands of pieces. It was too far away to see details but surely not even an Asgardian could survive that.

He turned away from the control panel. It was time to see how Dr. Selvig was doing with the portal stability device.

He got a little surprise then, in the form of quiet words from Agent Coulson. "You're going to lose."

"Am I?" Loki was intrigued. He paused to see what this dying mortal would have to say.

"It's in your nature."

Loki tried to understand what Coulson could possibly mean. "Your heroes are scattered, your floating fortress falls from the sky...where is my disadvantage?" he asked.

"You lack conviction," Coulson said. He did not move from where he sat against the wall. Blood trickled at the corner of his mouth, and the enormous gun lay uselessly across his lap.

Of all the things Coulson might have said, this was perhaps the one Loki expected least. *I have moved worlds out of conviction,* he thought. *Made bargains with beings who snuff out planets as an afterthought.* "I don't think I..."

The enormous gun discharged a bolt of dazzling blue energy, striking Loki squarely in the chest and blasting him through the nearest wall. For a moment, there was silence. Coulson watched, but Loki did not reappear.

Then he looked down at the gun. "So that's what it does," he said.

The Helicarrier wasn't quite in free fall, but it was close. It was losing altitude at a rate of hundreds of feet per minute, and unless Tony got the turbine going again, Steve knew they were all done for. The turbine was spinning faster, which was good, but the bad guys had just thrown a grenade at Steve and knocked him off the broken edge of the platform. He was hanging by a cable over a whole lot of air.

"Cap, hit the lever," Tony said.

"I need a minute here!" Steve shouted.

The turbine roared, reaching its full power. "Lever. Now!" Tony said, sounding more anxious. Then a sound came out of the turbine like the sound a garbage disposal makes when you drop a spoon into it.

Steve hauled his way back up the cable and dodged fire from Loki's men. He scrambled across the platform and pulled the lever.

Below the spinning turbine blades, vents opened. They were designed to keep the blades from overheating, but they also let Iron Man fall out. He tumbled a hundred feet or so before he got his boot thrusters under him. Then, accelerating, he arced back toward the Helicarrier. Steve watched him approach. What was he doing?

Oh. He blazed straight at the last of Loki's men and put him out of commission with a bone-crunching collision.

They were safe for the moment. The Helicarrier started to gain altitude again, and it leveled out. But a Quinjet was taking off, and Steve had a feeling Loki was on it. So they hadn't crashed, but they hadn't really won, either.

The final battle was yet to come.

CHAPTER 22

The Helicarrier was stabilized once Tony got the turbine going, but with Thor and the Hulk gone and Romanoff tied up with Barton, there was no way for the S.H.I.E.L.D. crew to stop Loki from escaping in the stolen Quinjet. All they could do was triage the wounded and do a head count to see how many they had lost. Nick Fury himself headed for the detention area, knowing that was where Coulson had been going.

He found Coulson sitting on the floor leaning against the wall. He was pale, his eyes heavy-lidded and his breath shallow. He looked up as Fury approached and knelt in front of him. Fury took the gun off his lap and set it on the floor.

"I'm sorry, boss. The god rabbited," Coulson said.

"Just stay awake. Eyes on me."

"No. I'm clocking out here." Even on the edge of death, Coulson kept his cool. Clocking out, Fury thought. How many soldiers could make a little joke in the last moments of their lives? Coulson was one of a kind.

"Not an option," Fury said. He couldn't afford to lose this man. Not after everything else they'd lost today.

"It's okay, boss," Coulson breathed. "This was never going to work...if they didn't have something...to..."

He never finished what he was going to say. With a last slow sigh, Agent Phil Coulson died. Nick Fury bowed his head. He'd lost plenty of men during his military career and plenty more with S.H.I.E.L.D....but this one hurt the most.

"Agent Coulson is down," he said over the intercom.

"A medical team is on its way to your location," said a dispatcher in return. But it was too late. Fury knew it was too late, and when the medical team arrived, they knew it, too.

If they didn't have something to...

That's right, Fury thought. Coulson was right. They needed something to pull them together, to make them see beyond themselves.

Now Fury was going to make sure they saw that. This battle had hurt them badly, but the war was not over. Not by a long shot.

A few hours later, after the casualties had been counted up and the first critical repairs were under way, Fury gathered the surviving members of the team in a conference room. Usually this was where he spoke remotely to the World Security Council, and he was looking forward to this conversation about as much as his meetings with them. Steve Rogers, Tony Stark, Natasha Romanoff, Maria Hill, and him. That was all that remained of the team. Loki had struck them a crippling blow.

But Fury wasn't ready to give up. He stood by the table near Steve Rogers and said, "These were in Phil Coulson's jacket. I guess he never did get you to sign them." He tossed bloodstained Captain America trading cards on the table. Rogers picked one of them up and looked at it. It was a picture of him from World War II, before he'd started going after Hydra in the mountains of northern Europe.

"We're dead in the air up here. Our communications, the location of the cube, Banner, Thor...I got nothing for you." He paused, trying not to get emotional. "I lost my one good eye," he added, meaning Coulson. "Maybe I had that coming."

No one else said anything. That was fine with Fury. He needed them to listen more than he needed a discussion.

"Yes," he said. "We were going to build an arsenal

with the Tesseract." There was no longer any reason to keep Phase Two a secret. Fury didn't regret hiding it from the team. It wouldn't have done them any good to know. "I never put all my chips on that number, though, because I was playing something even riskier," he went on. "There was an idea, Stark knows this, called the Avengers Initiative. The idea was to bring together a group of remarkable people to see if they could become something more. To see if they could work together when we needed them to, to fight the battles that we never could."

Tony was looking at him now, and Fury's next words were for Tony Stark and Tony Stark alone. "Phil Coulson died still believing in that idea," he said. "In heroes."

Tony suddenly got up. Fury thought for a moment that he was about to say something, but after a moment, he just left the bridge.

"Well," Fury said. "It's a good old-fashioned notion."

CHAPTER 23

Y ou fell out of the sky," a security guard said as Bruce recovered his senses.

He looked around. He was in a pile of rubble in what looked like a factory. Looking up, he saw a Hulk-size hole in the roof. "Did I hurt anybody?"

"There's nobody around here to get hurt," the guard said. Bruce could see his name tag. It read HARRY. "You did scare the hell out of some pigeons, though."

"Lucky," Bruce said. It was a funny thing to say when he was lying in a heap of broken concrete with no clothes on and no way to get back to the team, but it was true.

"Or just good aim," the guard said. "You were awake when you fell."

"You saw?"

"The whole thing. Right through the ceiling. Big and green and buck naked." He reached down and picked up a pair of pants. Tossing them to Bruce, he said, "Didn't think these would fit you until you shrunk down to a regular-size fellow."

"Thank you," Bruce said. He got the pants on. They were a little big, but a whole lot better than naked.

"Are you an alien?" the guard asked.

"What?"

"From outer space," the guard said. "An alien."

"No," Bruce said. He wasn't sure how to explain what he was, so he didn't try.

"Well then, son," the guard said, like he'd been thinking about it all night, "you've got a *condition*."

In a cell on the Helicarrier, Natasha Romanoff sat by Clint Barton's bed. He was restrained as a precautionary measure, because they had no way of knowing if they had really freed him of Loki's influence. Natasha thought she had seen him come back after she'd cracked his head into the catwalk railing but could not be sure...at least until she could talk to him for a minute. Then she would have to trust her instincts.

Barton thrashed at the restraints as he started to wake up. "Clint," Natasha said. "You're going to be all right."

She put a hand on his shoulder as he fought his way back to wakefulness. Barton got his eyes focused on her, and she knew he was back. She could see him in there instead of Loki...and she could see that he was scared and confused and angry.

"You know that?" he asked. "Is that what you know? I got...I gotta flush him out."

"You've got to level out," she said. "That's gonna take time."

He fell back on the bed. "You don't understand," he said. "Have you ever had someone take your brain and play? Take you out and stuff something else in? You know what it's like to be *unmade?*"

"You know that I do," she said. She'd been made and unmade more times than she could remember. She had told Loki as much when she said she was Russian...or used to be. Natasha didn't know what she was anymore, except that she was loyal to Nick Fury, loyal to S.H.I.E.L.D., and loyal to Clint Barton.

Barton looked over at her. "Why am I back? How'd you get him out?"

"Cognitive recalibration," she said, dead serious. Then with a small smile she explained. "I hit you really hard in the head."

He stared at her for a moment like he was trying to decide if she was joking. Then he just said, "Thanks."

That was what Natasha needed. She knew Barton was back. Now she could unbuckle his restraints.

He sat up, rubbing his wrists. "Tasha," he said. "How many agents did I—?"

"Don't," she said. "Don't do that to yourself, Clint. This is *Loki*. This is monsters and magic and nothing we were ever trained for." Better than maybe anyone on the Helicarrier, Natasha Romanoff knew you couldn't blame yourself for things you did while you were brainwashed. All you could do was try to heal and get things right the next time.

"Loki," Barton repeated. "He got away?"

"Yeah. Don't suppose you know where?"

He shook his head. "Didn't need to know. Didn't ask. He's gonna make his play soon, though. Today."

"We have to stop him," Natasha said.

"Yeah? Who's 'we'?"

"I don't know," she said. "Whoever's left."

Barton considered this. "Well," he said. "If I put an arrow through Loki's eye socket, I'd sleep better, I suppose."

She smiled. "Now you sound like you."

"But you don't," Barton said. "You're a spy, not

a soldier. Now you want to wade into a war. Why? What did Loki do to you?"

"He didn't, I just..." she trailed off, knowing she couldn't deceive Barton. Not after what he'd been through. He knew how Loki worked, how he got into your mind before you even knew it was happening.

"Natasha," he said, trying to get her to talk.

"I've been compromised," she said. Even though she'd known it, and used it to get information out of Loki, she still could feel the way he'd used her. "I got red in my ledger," she said, knowing Barton would understand. "I'd like to wipe it out."

CHAPTER 24

After Tony left the group, he found his way to the detention area where Loki had been held...and where Phil Coulson had died. He stood there thinking for a while, and then he noticed Steve Rogers had found his way there, too. Tony hoped Cap wasn't interested in picking up their argument where they'd left it off. He didn't have much stomach for a fight right then, at least not with Cap.

But Cap wasn't looking for a fight, either. He stood

for a minute, reflecting on what had happened in that room. Then he asked, "Was he married?"

"No," Tony said. "There was a, uh...cellist. I think." That was all he knew about Coulson's personal life, and he only knew that because of what he'd overheard when Pepper talked to Coulson. To Tony, Coulson had always been just an irritation, and now he was regretting that.

"I'm sorry. He seemed like a good man," Cap said.

"He was an idiot," Tony said.

"Why? For believing?"

"For taking on Loki alone," Tony said.

"He was doing his job," Cap insisted.

Cap's stubbornness made Tony angry. "He was out of his league," he said. "He should have waited. He should have..."

"Sometimes there isn't a way out, Tony," Cap said.

And there they were again, arguing over heroism. "Right," Tony said. "I've heard that before."

Cap walked toward him, not quite aggressive but definitely pressing his point. "Is this the first time you've lost a soldier?"

"We are not soldiers!" Tony said, barely keeping his voice below a shout. He was Tony Stark, billionaire genius! He was Iron Man! He was nobody's cannon fodder. "I am not marching to Fury's fife!"

"Neither am I! He's got the same blood on his hands that Loki does. But right now we've got to put that behind us and get this done. Loki needs a power source...." He stopped as he saw Tony's attitude change.

Tony had been struck by an idea. "He made it personal," he said.

"That's not the point," Cap said.

"That *is* the point," Tony insisted. "That's Loki's point! He hit us all right where we live. Why?"

Like he was talking to a child, Cap said, "To tear us apart."

"Yeah, divide and conquer is great, but he knows he has to take us out to win, right?" Now Tony was rolling. He had Loki figured out. "*That's* what he wants. He wants to beat us; he wants to be seen doing it. He wants an audience."

"Right. I caught his act at Stuttgart," Cap said.

"That was just previews," Tony said. "This is opening night. And Loki, he's a full-tilt diva, right? He wants flowers, he wants parades. He wants a monument built to the skies with his name plastered...."

That was it. Tony looked at Cap, and saw that he had figured it out, too. "Sonofagun," Tony said.

They both knew where Loki would strike next.

Erik Selvig had nearly completed the greatest scientific work of his life. The machine holding the Tesseract was complete, and ready for activation. It resembled the containment structure he had built in S.H.I.E.L.D.'s New Mexico facility, but he had made some improvements. This new machine was designed not to measure the Tesseract's power but to amplify and channel it. The Tesseract itself was the core of the machine. Around it was a plasma chamber and a conical array of mirrors and lenses. When the portal generator powered up, it would superheat the plasma in the chamber. Then the lenses would focus that energy into a beam that would tear open a hole in the universe and let the Chitauri through. Once that portal was open, Loki's triumph would be assured. No force on Earth would be able to oppose him.

He opened up his laptop—the same one he had used when he was working with Jane Foster, before they had ever seen Thor, or the Destroyer, or Loki. He ran through a series of software checks. Everything was in order. Soon, very soon, they would do something no human had ever dreamed of being able to do. Not even the Red Skull had understood the latent potential of the Tesseract.

And best of all, they would begin their conquest using Tony Stark's Arc Reactor in his magnificent new tower. Selvig looked out over the city of New York from the top of Stark Tower. By the end of the day, he thought, the world would be utterly transformed.

CHAPTER 25

If they were going after Loki, Steve knew they would need all hands on deck. He got dressed and headed down to the holding cell where Barton was recovering. At least Steve hoped he was recovering. He knew Natasha was there, and when he stuck his head in the door, he didn't bother with small talk. "Time to go," he said.

"Go where?" Natasha asked.

"Tell you on the way," Steve said. "Can you fly one of those jets?" Then he remembered that she'd been at the controls in Stuttgart. At the same time, he noticed that Barton wasn't in his bed. But before he had a chance to react, Barton walked into the room.

"I can," Barton said.

Steve glanced at Natasha, who gave him a subtle nod. Okay then, he thought. Barton's back with us. He had some questions, but this wasn't the time to ask them. It could all be sorted out later. If there was a later.

"Okay. Got a suit?" Steve asked.

Barton nodded.

"Then suit up."

An hour later, they were ready. Captain America, Hawkeye, and the Black Widow strode into a Quinjet, startling the S.H.I.E.L.D. tech doing maintenance. "I'm sorry, you guys aren't supposed to—"

"Son," Captain America said, "just don't."

Five minutes later, they were in the air.

Maria Hill needed to get something off her chest. She knew Fury had his own way of doing things, and usually that worked. But she didn't like being kept in the dark about operational planning. "Sir," she said, approaching him at his command station on the Helicarrier bridge.

"Agent Hill."

She stood next to him, and both of them looked out through the bridge windows. "Those cards. They were in Coulson's locker, not his pocket."

Fury nodded. "They needed the push."

"We have an unauthorized departure from base," a voice said over the intercom. At the same time, they saw a Quinjet launch, curving away to the north.

Toward New York City.

"They found it," Fury commented. "Get our communications back up, whatever you have to do. I want eyes on everything."

Maria Hill nodded. Fury had given her all the explanation she was going to get. "Yes, sir."

Tony Stark streaked over New York City, moving as fast as he could given the damage the Iron Man suit had suffered in the turbines. He sure wasn't at a 100 percent...but whatever he had would have to be good enough. "Sir, I've turned off the Arc Reactor, but the device is already self-sustaining," Jarvis said as Tony got close to Stark Tower. His home. His monument.

Now on the top floor stood a machine, perhaps eight feet tall. It was a rough cylinder with a focusing lens on the top, and below that, a chamber for containing the energies of the Tesseract. Dr. Erik Selvig stood watching it and also tracking data on a computer screen.

"Shut it down, Dr. Selvig," Tony said. He hovered ncar the machine, hoping Selvig wouldn't notice the way his thrusters were hiccupping. He was having trouble maintaining consistent thrust.

"It's too late!" Selvig cried. "She can't be stopped now! She wants to show us something! A new universe."

"Okay," Tony said. Clearly Selvig was beyond reason.

Tony blasted the machine with his repulsors, but it was surrounded by a force field of some kind. The reflected energy knocked him back and also sent Selvig and his computer flying across the rooftop.

"The barrier is pure energy," Jarvis said. "It's unbreakable."

"Yeah, I got that," Tony said. "Plan B." He saw Loki on the walkway that led from the landing pad into the penthouse.

"Sir, the Mark Seven is not ready for deployment," Jarvis said.

"Then skip the bells and whistles," Tony said. "We're on the clock." He sure couldn't take on Loki and the Chitauri, whatever they were, in the suit he was wearing. It was barely hanging together.

He landed and walked down the curving pathway toward Loki as the automated disassembly machinery took off his suit. Loki turned and went inside to meet him. Tony entered on the balcony level of the penthouse. From below, just inside the patio door, Loki greeted him. "Please tell me you're going to appeal to my humanity."

Tony came down the stairs and paused. "Uh, actually I'm planning to threaten you."

"You should have left your armor on for that," Loki said.

"Yeah, it's seen a bit of mileage, and you've got the Glow Stick of Destiny," Tony said with a shrug. He opened a decanter and held it up. "Would you like a drink?"

"Stalling me won't change anything," Loki said.

"No, no, no threatening!" Tony said. "No drink? You sure? I'm having one."

He poured himself a glass and swirled it before taking a small sip. Loki watched, cautious and intrigued, trying to see what Tony was planning.

"The Chitauri are coming," he said. "Nothing will change that. What have I to fear?"

"The Avengers," Tony said. He kept his tone chatty, casual, like they were talking about baseball scores or the weather. "That's what we call ourselves; we're sort of like a team. 'Earth's Mightiest Heroes' type of thing."

While he stoppered the decanter, he also slipped a bracelet over his wrist. Loki was looking the other way. The bracelet was a remote activator for the Mark 7 armor Jarvis was so worried about. Tony hoped he'd have a chance to use it…but with Loki, you never knew when things were going to go wrong.

"The Avengers," Loki said. "Yes, I've met them." His tone of voice left no doubt that he was unimpressed.

"Yeah, takes us a while to get any traction, I'll give you that one," Tony said. "But let's do a head count here. Your brother the demigod, a Super-Soldier, a living legend who kind of lives up to the legend, a man with breathtaking anger-management issues, a couple of master assassins…and you, big fella, you've managed to piss off every single one of them."

"That was the plan," Loki said with a grin.

"Not a great plan," Tony said. "When they come, and they will—"

Loki interrupted him. "I have an army."

"We have a Hulk," Tony said.

"I thought the beast had wandered off," Loki said, mocking him. And it was true that Tony had no idea where Bruce was. He was going on a wing and a prayer here, trusting that Bruce would show up again when they needed him.

"You're missing the point!" he said, and his tone got sharper. "There's no throne, there is no version of this where you come out on top. Maybe your army comes and maybe it's too much for us...but it's all on you. Because if we can't protect the Earth, you can be sure we'll avenge it."

He had stepped up to Loki, and now Loki closed the distance between them a little more. He had listened to Tony with a smile on his face, humoring him. Now he said, "How will your friends have time for me, when they're so busy fighting you?"

With those last words, he tapped Tony on the chest

with his scepter, just has he had Hawkeye and Dr. Selvig. Nothing happened. The Arc Reactor in Tony's chest countered the scepter's effect.

Loki tried it again. "This usually works...."

"Well," Tony said, "best-laid plans. You know the saying."

Suddenly angry, Loki flung Tony to the floor. "Jarvis," Tony said. "Anytime now."

Loki wrapped a hand around Tony's throat and lifted him to his feet. "You will all fall before me," he hissed.

"Deploy," Tony said. "Deploy!"

Lifting Tony into the air, Loki threw him through the window and over the balcony railing. Tony fell, watching the street rush up at him with incredible speed. If Jarvis was right and the Mark 7 wasn't ready, his part in the fight would be over really soon.

But you could never count Tony Stark out. The bracelet on his wrist chirped, and the Mark 7 armor burst out of a closet, rocketing down after Tony. Keyed to the bracelet's homing signal, it reached him in midair. The armor opened up and built itself around his body while Tony fell. He engaged its thrusters less than fifty feet above the ground, and with a big grin on his face, Tony rocketed back up to have a little word with Loki.

Nobody threw him off his own roof.

He got to the balcony and saw a very surprised Loki. "There's one other person I forgot to mention," Tony said. "His name is Phil."

And he blew Loki across the room with a repulsor blast.

CHAPTER 26

Above Tony Stark and Loki, on the rooftop, the Tesseract activated. A beam of blue energy pierced the sky—literally. It opened a hole fifty thousand feet above New York. On the other side of that hole was space...and the waiting Chitauri. They began to pour through, riding small machines like flying motorcycles. There were dozens of them at first, then hundreds, racing down toward the city that lay defenseless below.

Or at least, Tony thought, the Chitauri thought it was defenseless. He flew up to meet them. Somewhere—he hoped not too far away—the rest of the team was coming. It sure was going to be a long day if he had to take on the entire Chitauri invading force by himself, in a suit that had never even been tested in the field.

As fast as he could, Tony blasted the Chitauri out of the air with repulsors and shoulder-mounted mini-missiles. There were too many of them! They got past him and flew low over the streets of New York, shooting wildly and destroying anything in their path.

The Battle of New York had begun.

Newly transformed into his Asgardian armor and helmet, Loki watched. At last, his conquest was beginning.

Then, for the second time in a few minutes, he was unpleasantly surprised by the appearance of someone he had thought dead.

Thor dropped out of the sky to land on Tony's balcony. "Loki!" he roared. "Turn off the Tesseract or I'll destroy it!"

"You can't!" Loki cried out, riding a wave of exhilaration at seeing his army finally in action. "There is no stopping it. There is only...the war!"

"So be it," Thor growled.

Loki jumped down from the rooftop and slashed at Thor with the scepter. Thor blocked it and struck back with Mjolnir. They battled with the fury that only brothers at war can feel, their combat tearing pieces away from the top of Stark Tower to fall onto the roofs of shorter buildings nearby.

Around them, the Chitauri army marauded through the streets. New York was rapidly falling into chaos.

The Quinjet was coming in hot with Barton at the controls and Natasha monitoring the situation...which didn't look so good. She saw Iron Man zigzagging through the city and broke radio silence to let him know they were close. "Stark, we're on your three, headed northeast," Natasha said.

"What, did you stop for drive-through? Swing up Park Avenue, I'm going to lay them out for you." A large group of Chitauri were right on Tony's tail. He angled north and then banked back around. The Chitauri followed, and the Quinjet caught them from the side, shooting many of them down with its belly-mounted cannon.

"Sir, we have more incoming," Jarvis said.

"Fine. Let's keep 'em occupied," Tony said.

The Quinjet swung by Stark Tower, still firing as the Chitauri air bikes came within range. Hawkeye saw Thor and Loki fighting. He gestured to the Black Widow. "Nat?"

"I see them."

Hawkeye brought the Quinjet around and slowed it to a near hover so she could target Loki—but before the Quinjet's gun locked in, Loki got off a bolt of energy from his scepter. It exploded in the Quinjet's left wing engine, sending the jet into a violent downward spiral. Only Hawkeye's superb piloting skills kept them from crashing straight down and taking most of a building with them. As it was, they landed hard in a street-side plaza a few blocks from Stark Tower. Quickly, they unbuckled and got out of the Quinjet, with Captain America in the lead. "We need to get back up there," he said.

They ran toward Stark Tower as the Chitauri flashed overhead, strafing the streets. Tony was shooting them down as fast as he could, but there were still plenty left. And then a groaning noise came from the hole in the sky, and they looked up to see a giant creature coming through from Chitauri space.

It was hundreds of feet long, with a gaping mouth and a tail that undulated up and down as it seemed to swim through the air. It had no wings. It had fins, and bony spikes sticking up from its back. It was like a giant skeletal fish that could fly, and it bore down on New York. As it dove between the skyscrapers of Midtown, portals in its sides opened, and Chitauri foot soldiers leaped out, hanging onto the sides of buildings and breaking in through the windows.

"Stark, are you seeing this?" Cap radioed.

"Seeing. Still working on believing," Tony answered. He was hot on the Leviathan's tail, but he had no idea how to fight something that big. A flick of its armored body destroyed whole floors of buildings. "Where's Banner? Has he shown up yet?"

"Banner?" Cap echoed.

"Just keep me posted," Tony said. They were going to need Bruce before this was all over. He flew in parallel with the Leviathan, wondering what to do next. "Jarvis, find me a soft spot," he said. Jarvis got to work.

But while he did that, Tony was going to have to distract the monster before it wrecked the city all by itself.

He made a pass in front of the Leviathan and speckled its head with minimissiles. They didn't hurt it, but it turned to come after him with a roar that shook bricks loose from nearby storefronts. "Well, we got its attention. What was step two?" he wondered aloud as he accelerated away.

CHAPTER 27

ook at this!" Thor shouted, holding Loki and forcing him to gaze out over the destruction in the city. "You think this madness will end with your rule?"

"It's too late," Loki said. Thor thought he was beginning to understand what he had done. "It's too late to stop it."

"No," Thor said. "We can. Together."

Loki looked him in the eye...and then betrayed Thor again, stabbing him in the side with a knife hidden in his sleeve. Thor dropped to the ground, clutching the wound. "Sentiment," Loki said mockingly.

Enraged, Thor got to his feet and pounded Loki through the window. Then he lifted him up and slammed him to the stone balcony. He was beyond talking now, and Loki knew he was in trouble. He looked to his scepter, but it was out of reach, so he rolled to the edge of the balcony and let himself fall.

Thor rushed to the edge and looked down. Loki fell...and landed on a passing Chitauri flying machine. Piloting it, he sped away, leaving Thor alone on top of Stark Tower.

On a bridge, Cap huddled behind a destroyed car with the Black Widow and Hawkeye. "Lots of civilians trapped up there," Hawkeye said, indicating the nearby buildings. A flight of Chitauri went over, and Cap noticed something different about one of them.

"Loki," he said. He was shooting at the civilians fleeing through the streets. "They're fish in a barrel down there."

Chitauri foot soldiers dropped onto the bridge and advanced toward them. "We're good," Natasha said. "Go."

"You think you can hold them off?" Steve asked.

Hawkeye glanced over his shoulder as he nocked an arrow. "Captain, it would be my genuine pleasure."

They swung into action. Cap sprinted down the street in pursuit of Loki while Hawkeye and the Black Widow started taking down the Chitauri and freeing trapped civilians. On the street level, Cap dodged explosions. "Just like Budapest all over again," Natasha said as she shot down a pair of Chitauri trying to get behind them.

"You and I remember Budapest very differently," Barton said.

Steve got to the police lines. They were firing at the Chitauri and holding their ground, but they were clearly overwhelmed. He heard one of them say it would be an hour before the military could arrive. "Do they know what's going on here?" a second cop said.

The first cop looked up at the Leviathan. "Do we?"

Steve vaulted over a line of destroyed vehicles and landed on top of a taxi. The police pointed their guns at him, but he ignored that. "You need men in these buildings. There are people inside, and they're going to be running right into the line of fire. You take them to the basements, or through the subway. You keep them off the streets. I need a perimeter as far back as Thirty-Ninth."

The sergeant looked at him like he'd just escaped from the loony bin. "Why the hell should I take orders from you?"

Steve didn't have time to argue about it, because

at that moment, the Chitauri attacked. Their flyers swooped low and dropped ground troops close to the police line. Steve blocked a blast with his shield and in the same motion batted away the closest Chitauri. He pivoted and brought the shield up to parry a spear thrust from another Chitauri, knocking it down with a single punch and then grabbing its spear. He slashed a third Chitauri down with the weapon, and without breaking stride, lunged forward to grapple with a fourth and beat it into submission before throwing it back off the roof of the taxi.

Without another word to Steve, the police sergeant started calling orders into his radio. "I need men in those buildings," he said, pointing so all his officers could see. "Lead the people down and away from the streets. We're going to set up a perimeter all the way down Thirty-Ninth Street."

Steve didn't stop to gloat. There was a war to win.

He got back together with Hawkeye and the Black Widow. The three of them took Chitauri down as fast as guns, bow, and shield could do it. Even so, they were close to being overwhelmed—until lightning struck out of a clear blue sky, decimating the Chitauri in the area.

Thor dropped down to land in front of them. He looked wounded, tired...and as angry as any of them had ever seen a man look.

In that moment, Steve was glad he wasn't a Chitauri. And he was especially glad he wasn't Loki. "So what's the story upstairs?" he asked.

"The power surrounding the cube is impenetrable," Thor said.

"Thor's right," Tony said as he zipped by overhead. "You've got to deal with these guys."

"How do we do this?" Natasha asked.

"As a team," Steve said.

Thor was still watching the Chitauri zipping overhead. "I have unfinished business with Loki."

"Yeah?" Hawkeye said. "Get in line."

"Save it," Steve said. "Loki's going to keep this fight focused on us, and that's what we need. Otherwise those things could run wild. We've got Stark up on top—"

He broke off as a motorcycle engine approached,

idling down. Steve glanced over and saw the welcome sight of Bruce Banner. "So," Bruce said. "This all seems horrible."

"I've seen worse," the Black Widow said.

He knew what she meant. "Sorry."

"No," she said. "We could use a little worse."

"Stark," Steve said into his mic. "We got him."

"Banner?" Tony said.

Steve nodded. "Just like you said."

"Then tell him to suit up," Tony said. "I'm bringing the party to you."

A moment later, they saw Iron Man swoop around a corner to their north...and right behind him, the gargantuan armored Leviathan, shattering the corner building as it made the turn in pursuit. "I...I don't see how that's a party," Natasha said.

Iron Man dropped almost down to street level, and the Leviathan followed, smashing cars and streetlights out of the way as it bore down on the group of heroes. "Dr. Banner," Steve said. "Now might be a really good time for you to get angry."

Bruce was already walking toward the Leviathan.

"That's my secret, Captain," he said over his shoulder. "I'm always angry."

When he turned back to face the Leviathan, his transformation was already beginning. He grew, his clothes shredding away from his body as ordinary Bruce Banner became the eight-foot-tall, two-thousand-pound mass of invincible rage called the Hulk. As the Leviathan ducked its head toward him, the Hulk brought his fist down on the creature's head with a booming crunch that shook the bridge the Avengers stood on. The Leviathan's head dug into the road surface, plowing up chunks of concrete. Its momentum shoved the Hulk back, but he stopped himself as the rest of the Leviathan's body toppled up and over them. It crashed to the street below and lay still.

All over the city, the Chitauri stopped and screeched in sudden shock, as if they had never imagined the great beast could be defeated. The Avengers looked around. All six of them were together as a group for the first time in combat. Maybe the tide was beginning to turn, Steve thought.

Then Natasha, looking up into the sky, said, "Guys?"

They all looked. More Chitauri poured through the portal...and more Leviathans. What they had thought was the climactic battle had in fact just been the beginning.

CHAPTER 28

Call it, Captain!" Iron Man said.

"All right, listen up," Steve said. "Until we can close that portal, our priority's containment. Barton, I want you on that roof, eyes on everything. Call out patterns and strays. Stark, you got the perimeter. Anything gets more than three blocks out, you turn it back or you turn it to ash."

Hawkeye turned to Iron Man. "Want to give me a lift?"

"Right," Iron Man said. He wrapped an arm around Hawkeye's waist. "Better clench up." He rocketed straight up to the rooftop Steve had pointed out, and released Hawkeye before taking off to hold the perimeter around Stark Tower.

"Thor," Steve went on, "you have to try to bottleneck that portal. Slow 'em down. You got the lightning. Light the bastards up."

Thor swung Mjolnir in a tight circle and flew off, smashing Chitauri out of his way as he rose higher against the New York City skyline. Steve turned to the Black Widow. "You and me, we stay here on the ground, keep the fighting here," he said. "And, Hulk?"

The Hulk turned and glowered at Steve.

There was really only one order you could give the Hulk, Steve thought. One word. "Smash."

The Hulk bared his teeth and leaped away. He bounded up the sides of nearby buildings, crushing Chitauri with single blows whenever he was in arm's reach of them. Then he leaped into the air and swatted their flyers down before charging off into the chaos.

Thor reached the top of the Empire State Building and lifted Mjolnir. Storm clouds gathered and lightning struck down, hundreds of bolts reaching for Mjolnir. Thor turned the Empire State Building's iconic spire into a lightning rod, gathering the force of the elements into it. Then he thrust Mjolnir in the direction of the portal. All the energy he had built up blazed out in a single forking bolt. It struck and destroyed every single Chitauri between the Empire State Building and the portal itself. Hundreds of them exploded and tumbled from the sky at once, including several of the Leviathans that tumbled down to smash into buildings below.

He had earned them a breather, but only for a moment. It was up to the rest of the Avengers to put it to good use and turn the tide against Loki.

On the Helicarrier, Fury and Hill watched. She cocked her head and listened as a message came over her earbud. "Sir? The Council is on."

This was the last thing Fury needed in the middle of a war. But he turned to answer the call.

From his sniper's perch, Hawkeye shot arrow after arrow, every one finding its mark. He also tried to keep an eye on what threats the rest of the team was facing. "Stark? Got a lot of strays sniffing your tail."

"Just trying to keep them off the streets," Tony joked.

"Well, they can't bank the way you can," Hawkeye said. "You might want to find a tight corner."

"I will roger that," Tony said.

Hawkeye watched as Iron Man peeled his Chitauri pursuers off in a series of maneuvers through tight spaces. They crashed into overpasses and blew up, or spun out of control trying to stay with Iron Man through tight turns between tall buildings. The last of them lit up the front of a bank building with a fireball and Tony said, "Nice call. What else you got?"

"Well," Hawkeye said, "Thor's taking on a squadron down on Sixth."

"And he didn't invite me," Tony said in mock anger.

That's the attitude, Hawkeye thought.

The Hulk charged through a building, leaping out the window to land on the muzzle of an approaching Leviathan before it could tear the building down. Workers screamed as he pulled it around to the side and down, hammering away at its armor-plated skull.

He brought it down to the street and finished it off, not far from where the Black Widow and Captain America were holding their own against overwhelming numbers of Chitauri on foot. They couldn't do it forever.

"Captain," the Black Widow said, "none of this is going to mean a thing if we don't close that portal."

"Our biggest guns couldn't touch it," Cap said.

"Well, maybe it's not about guns," she suggested.

Steve thought he knew what she was getting at. She

was mighty good in close quarters. "If you want to get up there, you're gonna need a ride," he said.

She eyed a passing Chitauri flyer. "I can get a ride. I could use a boost, though."

"Are you sure about this?" he asked.

She looked up, gauging the distance and speed of an oncoming flyer. "Yeah. It's gonna be fun."

She ran and leaped onto his shield, and Steve flung her into the air. She caught the bottom of the Chitauri craft and was gone, riding it out of sight.

Iron Man saw her fly past and figured he might know what she was up to. He picked off the nearest Chitauri following her and then peeled back to give Cap a hand. He was all by himself facing down maybe twenty Chitauri. Tony hit the ground firing and evened the odds a little. He still hadn't found Thor's little party that Hawkeye had mentioned.

That was because Thor and the Hulk were on the back of a Leviathan. The Hulk wrenched loose one of its dorsal plates, reared back, and pounded it into the base of the Leviathan's skull. Thor followed with a blow from Mjolnir and the Leviathan heeled over to one side. They smashed through the windows of a train station's upper level and came to rest. Satisfied, Thor nodded and glanced over at the Hulk. Perhaps the scales were evened from their last fight against each other on the Helicarrier—

The Hulk shot out his left fist and smashed Thor all the way across the block-long gallery. Then it was his turn to look satisfied.

Very well, Thor thought. *Now we're even. Let us take the fight to the Chitauri, and to Loki!*

CHAPTER 29

Steve was taking down Chitauri as fast as he could. There were always more of them. He fought with everything he had, from the streets near the train station to a bank where he freed a roomful of hostages...but when that fight was over, he stood in the street and thought maybe they weren't going to win after all. The military had arrived, but all they could do was coordinate evacuations and provide a little covering fire. They couldn't mount an effective opposition to the Chitauri. Steve stood and for a moment he felt something he'd never felt before.

Hopeless.

Maybe that was just Loki, but Steve was starting to feel like the Chitauri were going to absorb every punch the Avengers could throw. They had to close that portal, or nothing was going to stop the invasion.

Fury stood and listened to the World Security Council explain that they had decided to take the operation out of his hands. They were going to use a nuclear missile to destroy the Tesseract and close the portal—but at the cost of untold civilian lives. Fury protested as strongly as he could and one of the councilors cut him off. "Director Fury. The Council has made a decision."

"I recognize the Council has made a decision," Fury said. "But given that it's a stupid decision, I've elected to ignore it."

"Director, you're closer than any of our subs. You scramble that jet."

"That is the island of Manhattan, Councilor. Until I am certain my men cannot hold it, I will not order a nuclear strike against a civilian population."

"If we don't hold them here, we lose everything."

That's what you don't understand, Fury thought. "If I send that bird out, we already have."

Natasha was having trouble shaking the last Chitauri pursuing her. When she glanced over her shoulder, she understood why.

It was Loki.

"Hawkeye," she said, pulling her craft into a tight turn back toward his position. He was still on the rooftop where Iron Man had dropped him, across the street from Stark Tower, and he was still picking Chitauri out of the sky with his incredible accuracy.

"I got him," he said. He lined up an arrow and let it fly.

It was an incredible shot, over a distance of several hundred yards at a moving target, and it was perfect—until Loki reached up and snatched the arrow out of the air just inches from his face. He looked in Hawkeye's direction and smiled. . . .

And that was when the explosive arrowhead detonated and blew him off the Chitauri craft.

He fell onto the Stark Tower balcony as the out-of-control craft destroyed the *S* and the *T* in the Stark logo. Thor had already inadvertently smashed the *R* before.

The Black Widow followed, leaping off her craft and rolling into a combat stance. Loki saw her and stood. She knew she didn't have a chance against him in a straight-up fight, but that wasn't going to stop her from trying.

But she never got the chance. The Hulk, flying out of nowhere, crashed into Loki and drove him through the last intact balcony window into Tony's living room. He pounded the floor and came after Loki again, but Loki stood up and screamed, "Enough!"

The Hulk paused, confused.

"You are, all of you, beneath me!" Loki raged. "I am a god, you dull creature, and I will not be bullied by—"

The Hulk didn't bother to listen to anymore. He grabbed Loki's leg, swung the Asgardian over his head, and pounded him down into the floor six or seven times as hard as he could. When it was over, the floor was trashed and so was Loki. He lay staring up at the ceiling, an expression of incredible surprise on his face.

"Puny god," the Hulk snarled, and stomped off to rejoin the fight.

On the rooftop, Natasha approached the machine holding the Tesseract, wondering what she could do. "The scepter," said Erik Selvig. She looked over at him and saw that he was free of Loki's spell. How had that happened? She knew Iron Man had tried to destroy the machine. Maybe the explosion from his repulsors had shocked Selvig back to his senses, just like Hawkeye had been freed from Loki by a sharp blow to the head.

"What about it?" she asked.

"The energy. The Tesseract can't fight it. You can't protect against yourself." He was wracked with guilt, she could see it on his face. Again, just like Barton. Both of them were suffering from the knowledge of what they had done under Loki's control.

She knelt next to him and said, "It's not your fault. You didn't know what you were doing."

Selvig digested this for a moment and then said, "Actually I think I did. I built in a safety to cut the power source."

"Loki's scepter," she said, understanding. The scepter was given its power by the same source as the Tesseract. It could reach through the energy barrier!

"Maybe it will close the portal," he said, and glanced down over the edge of the rooftop to a lower floor. "And I'm looking right at it."

Elsewhere on the battlefield, the Chitauri were slowly but surely gaining the upper hand. There were just too many of them, thousands and thousands—against only six Avengers. Hawkeye ran out of arrows and was forced to flee his rooftop sniper's perch. Iron Man's energy was running desperately low after he destroyed another Leviathan by flying into its mouth and exploding it from the inside on his way through. Captain America was battered and at the edge of his strength.

And in a hangar on the Helicarrier, a pilot was receiving orders: *"Director Fury is no longer in command. Override order seven alpha one one."*

"Seven alpha one one confirmed," the pilot said. "We're go for takeoff."

He lifted off, carrying a nuclear missile designed to put an end to the Chitauri threat once and for all...but it would also be the end of every living thing on the island of Manhattan.

On the bridge, Maria Hill called out, "We have a rogue bird! Someone stop it!"

Nick Fury himself ran out onto the flight deck with a shoulder-fired missile launcher. He blew the landing gear out from under the taxiing jet, and it skidded to a halt on the edge of the deck...but then a second jet screamed past, taking off before he could do anything about it.

The World Security Council had gone behind his back. And they had sent two planes anticipating he would be able to react fast enough to get one.

Now it didn't make any difference, unless...Fury got on the radio and pinged Iron Man directly, not wanting to distract the rest of the team. "Stark. Do you hear me? You have a missile headed straight for the city."

The sounds of battle crackled back through the radio along with Tony Stark's voice. "How long?"

"Three minutes, max," Fury said. "The payload will wipe out Midtown. At least."

Tony didn't ask any more questions. "Jarvis, put everything we've got into the thrusters," Fury heard him say. When he got back inside to the bridge, he could see that Iron Man had shed his Chitauri pursuit and rocketed away from the battle, heading south to intercept the missile.

CHAPTER 30

On the rooftop, Natasha had the scepter. She pushed the tip against the energy barrier protecting the portal generator. It went through, slowly. "I can close it," she said, hoping she could be heard over the wash of electromagnetic energy from the barrier. "Can anybody copy? I can shut the portal down!"

"Do it!" Captain America replied immediately.

But as she leaned on the scepter to push it the rest

of the way through to the Tesseract itself, Iron Man broke in. "No, wait!"

"Stark, these things are still coming!" Cap argued.

"I got a nuke coming in," Tony answered. "It's going to blow in less than a minute, and I know just where to put it."

Natasha looked around. She couldn't see Tony.... No, there he was, far away to the south, the contrail of his boot thrusters leading away from the battle. A nuke, she thought. Fury wouldn't have done that. The only people on Earth who would turn Manhattan into a radioactive crater—other than various terrorist groups and lunatic super villains—were the World Security Council. They had to be behind this.

She waited, holding the scepter in place. If anyone could pull this off, it would be Tony Stark...but Natasha wasn't sure anyone could pull this off.

Tony caught the missile right after it went under the Verrazano-Narrows Bridge. He had to time everything perfectly or he would either miss the portal or not get to it in time. He rode the missile north, streaking over Battery Park, the Financial District, Little Italy, Chinatown, the Village...then he started trying to force it higher into the sky, away from its target location over Midtown Manhattan—and toward the hole in space created by the Tesseract.

The missile had a lot of momentum built up, and Tony's Mark 7 suit was not operating at full capacity after the amount of energy he'd expended in the battle already. It was no easy task to get the missile angled up sharply enough to clear the tallest buildings in Midtown—especially Stark Tower. That was where the missile seemed to want to go. *So,* Tony thought, *the World Security Council is jealous of me, too.*

He got underneath the missile and angled it upward, straining against its stabilizers, which tried to keep it on course. But slowly he forced it up, and once he got its warhead pointed at an angle, pushing it into a steeper climb got easier. A little.

Steve Rogers's voice broke his concentration. "Stark, you know that's a one-way trip?"

Tony ignored him. If he talked to Steve, he was going to think too much about how Steve was probably right. "Save the rest for the turn, J," he said to Jarvis once the missile was pointed in the right direction.

"Sir, shall I try Ms. Potts?" Jarvis asked.

"Might as well," Tony said. She was probably busy with some congressional thing or other, but maybe he could leave her a message.

Tony and the missile passed within feet of the roof of Stark Tower, close enough that he could see the amazement on the faces of Natasha and Selvig. Then he fired extra lateral thrusters and aimed the missile straight up, adding his own thrust to the missile's solid-fuel engine and blazing toward the portal. Pepper's phone kept ringing, but she didn't answer. The portal loomed ahead, with more Chitauri appearing through it all the time. As Tony got closer, he could see more clearly what was on the other side.

Empty space. Stars. And lots and lots of Chitauri.

This better work, he thought, and then he was through the portal.

Jarvis cut out as the wireless link to Stark Tower was

broken. The call to Pepper failed. His thrusters flickered and began to go out. Tony let go of the missile and fell back toward the portal. His eyes were wide.

Against a backdrop of alien stars, the Chitauri ship hung in space. It was bigger than anything he had ever seen, shaped like a rough X lying on its side. Any one of the legs of the X was larger than a dozen Helicarriers. Leviathans poured from it, and Chitauri flyers swarmed like dust. They would just keep coming, in their thousands and millions, if it wasn't destroyed. What kind of a civilization could build something like that? Humans were centuries away from that kind of technology. Fury was right. When it came to threats from space, the human race was hilariously outgunned. All they could do was hope that brains and willpower would even the odds.

The missile streaked on toward it, its timer ticking down. Tony watched. Even if this was the last thing he ever saw, part of him was glad that he had seen it. The universe was full of wonders. One day, Tony knew, the human race would make it out among the stars . . . but first they would have to stay alive long enough.

That meant defeating the Chitauri.

A tiny ball of fire bloomed in the center of the Chitauri ship. It grew and kept growing. In seconds, it had engulfed the Chitauri ship.

Tony closed his eyes.

On the streets of New York, the Chitauri fell to the ground as if they had been switched off. Every single one of them. Even the remaining Leviathans sagged and crashed to earth.

The Avengers looked up. On the roof of Stark Tower, Natasha said, "Come on, Stark."

They saw the explosion through the portal, brilliant as a new sun. There was no way Tony could have survived that.

I was wrong about him, Steve thought. When the time came, he did make the sacrificial play. "Close it," he said. There was nothing they could do for Tony now.

Natasha leaned in and touched the tip of Loki's

scepter to the Tesseract. The beam of energy holding the portal open winked out and the portal began to collapse. All the Avengers watched, knowing they had lost one of their own.

Then, at the last minute before the portal winked out of existence, the minuscule form of Iron Man fell through it back into the sky.

"Sonofagun," Steve said.

Smiles spread across their faces. Tony was alive!

But soon they could tell something wasn't right. "He's not slowing down," Thor said. He started to swing Mjolnir, to fly up and intercept Tony before he could hit the ground at a fatal velocity.

He never got the chance, though, because the Hulk came leaping into view. He caught Iron Man, and his momentum carried him all the way across to the building across the street. Using one hand to slow himself, he slid down the building's facade to the street. When they came to rest, the Hulk dropped Iron Man on the ground and bent over him. Thor and Steve came running. "Is he breathing?" Steve asked.

Thor ripped the face mask off the Iron Man armor.

Tony didn't move. His miniature Arc Reactor was dark.

They stood for a long moment, realizing that they had lost him after all. The portal was collapsed. The Chitauri were gone or deactivated. Tony Stark had sacrificed himself to save humanity.

Then, just to be sure, the Hulk bent low and roared in Tony's face.

The sound was earsplitting from down the block; Steve thought it must have been just about able to wake the dead up close. Tony gasped and his eyes shot open. "What?! What just happened? Please tell me nobody kissed me."

The Hulk grunted. Steve cracked a smile. Even in a moment like this, Tony had to make a joke. "We won," he said.

"All right," Tony said. He had started to sit up, but now he lay back again. "Yay. All right. Good job, guys. Let's just not come in tomorrow. Let's just take a day." He rested, getting his breath for a minute. Then he started talking again. "Have you ever tried shawarma? There's a shawarma joint about two blocks from here. I don't know what it is, but I wanna try it."

"Shawarma," Steve said. He had no idea what it was, either. For once, he and Tony were both in the dark about something. "Sure, why not."

"We're not finished yet," Thor said.

"Oh, okay," Tony said. "Then shawarma after."

CHAPTER 31

Loki had just gotten himself put back together enough to get out of the hole in the floor. Painfully he dragged himself toward the door. Never had a mortal damaged him as much as that green monster. He would be healing for a long time. But heal he would, and then he would have his revenge. Even though the portal had collapsed and he had lost the Tesseract. Even though his Chitauri army was destroyed. Loki would show the so-called Avengers they never should have opposed him.

He heard a noise behind him and rolled over … and there they stood. All of them. Even the ones he'd thought dead. Thor, Iron Man, Hawkeye, Captain America, the Hulk, and the Black Widow. She even held Loki's scepter, adding to the indignity.

Loki sighed. He knew when he was defeated—at least for the moment. "If it's all the same to you," he said, "I'll have that drink now."

The Avengers met one last time to make sure Loki, Thor, and the Tesseract got off Earth and back to Asgard. Then they shook hands and dispersed, each knowing that if the need arose, Nick Fury would know how to find them. On the Helicarrier, with repair crews swarming the damaged turbine and the collapsed interior decks, Nick Fury held off the World Security Council as long as he could, wanting to give the Avengers a head start. But eventually he had to answer the Council's call . . . and they were not happy.

They demanded to know how Iron Man had discovered the inbound missile. Fury told them. Enraged, they then demanded that the Avengers be brought together and kept in one place under World Security Council supervision.

"I'm afraid I can't do that," Fury said.

"Where are the Avengers?" the lead councilor asked.

"I'm not currently tracking their whereabouts," Fury answered. "I'd say they've earned a leave of absence."

This wasn't strictly true. He was tracking their whereabouts and knew they had gathered to see Thor and Loki off back to Asgard . . . with the Tesseract. He also knew that once the Asgardians were gone, Tony, Bruce, Natasha, Barton, and Steve would scatter to the four winds.

Exactly as Fury wanted them. The farther apart they were, the harder it would be for the councilors to keep an eye on them. Fury was an old dog who knew lots of tricks. One of them was that he knew better than to trust groups like the World Security Council. After all, they'd already gone behind his back and tried to nuke Manhattan.

"And the Tesseract?" the councilor pressed.

"The Tesseract is where it belongs: out of our reach." Right about then, Fury guessed, Thor and Loki would be gripping the handles of a cylindrical case holding the Tesseract. They were using its power to return to Asgard, since they couldn't use the Bifrost.

"That's not your call," the councilor said ominously.

"I didn't make it," Fury said. "I just didn't argue with the god that did."

"So you let him take it and the war criminal, Loki, who should be answering for his crimes?"

"Oh, I think he will be," Fury said. He didn't know what Asgardian justice was like, but he had a feeling Loki wasn't going to like it. The last time he'd seen Thor's brother, Loki had been fitted out with a steel half mask that held his mouth shut. Unless Fury was badly mistaken, it would be a long time before Loki would be able to sweet-talk anyone into anything again.

The councilor wasn't ready to let it go. "I don't think you understand what you've started, letting the Avengers loose on this world. They're dangerous."

"They surely are," Fury agreed. "And the whole world knows it. Every world knows it."

"That the point of all this? A statement?"

Nick Fury leaned a little closer to the holographic silhouettes of all the members of the World Security Council. "A promise," he said.

He broke off the call and returned to the Helicarrier's bridge. There was a lot to do before this ship would be combat-ready again, and no telling how much time they had. The world—the worlds—were full of threats.

"Sir, how does it work now?" Maria Hill asked from her station. "They've gone their separate ways, some pretty far. We get into a situation like this again, what happens then?"

"They'll come back," Fury said.

"Are you really sure about that?"

Fury nodded. "I am."

"Why?"

"Because we'll need them to," Nick Fury said simply. Then he got back to work.

TURN THE PAGE FOR AN EXCITING PREVIEW OF

MARVEL CINEMATIC UNIVERSE
PHASE ONE

MARVEL

CAPTAIN AMERICA
THE FIRST AVENGER

Walking inside the recruitment center, Steve Rogers was directed to an examination room. His eyes quickly adjusted to the dark. Where outside it was all bright lights and noisy crowds, inside it was quiet and somber. Out of the corner of his eye, Steve saw an older man come in. He looked tired, as though being there took all his energy.

The man made his way slowly over to Steve. "So. You want to go overseas? Be a hero?" he asked in a

German accent. Steve just looked at him. He wasn't sure what to say. Was this some kind of test?

"Dr. Abraham Erskine," the man said, introducing himself. "Strategic Scientific Reserve, US Army."

Steve had never heard of the Strategic Scientific Reserve but figured there were a lot of things he hadn't heard of. Shrugging, he gave Erskine his name and looked on as the man found his file. Steve tried not to grimace when he once again saw all the red x's, marking each and every one of his ailments and weaknesses.

"Where are you from?" he asked, to draw the doctor's attention away from the file.

"Queens," Erskine said. He paused, then added, "Before that, Germany. This bothers you?"

Steve was momentarily taken aback. Was this place legit? He hadn't expected a German national to be inside a US Army recruitment center.

Then again, wasn't Einstein German, too? "No," he said, but he hesitated first.

It didn't seem to bother Erskine. Probably he'd heard it all before. He finished reviewing the file and then looked up. "Where are you from, Mr. Rogers?" he asked. "Hmm? New Haven? Or is it..." He glanced down at the file again. "Paramus...Newark...five exams in five tries in five different cities," he said. "All failed. You are very tenacious, yes?"

How did he know that? Steve wondered. He'd thought that by going to different cities, he could stay under the radar and the army wouldn't see how desperate he was to enlist. Maybe this Strategic Scientific Reserve, whatever it was, had more intel than the other branches of the army.

Outside, a pair of men wandered by and turned when they heard Erskine's German accent. They took a step forward as though to do something, when Steve held up a warning hand. Figuring it wasn't worth it, they moved on.

"A fella has to stand up," Steve said, turning back to Erskine. "I don't like bullies, Doc. I don't care where they're from."

The old man nodded thoughtfully. "So you would fight, yes," he said. "But you are weak and you are very small."

Steve was about to protest, when Dr. Erskine did something unexpected: He laid out Steve's file on the table and picked up a stamp. Steve's heart began to beat faster.

"I can offer you a chance," Dr. Erskine said. "Only a chance."

Then, as Steve watched with growing excitement, the man pressed the stamp down on the file. Holding up the file, Steve saw a big *1A*.

He couldn't believe it. After all this time, he was actually in the army. His luck *had* changed. Just like he told Bucky it would.

As Erskine began talking about next steps, Steve tried to pay attention. But his mind was spinning. He had no idea what kind of group the SSR was or why they would okay someone like him. Should he be worried? Was Bucky right when he said the biggest danger would come if someone *did* let him in? What if this was all some sort of joke? Maybe when he got outside he'd see Bucky laughing, having pulled a fast one on his old friend.

Shaking off those thoughts, Steve focused on Erskine. Whatever the SSR was and whatever the reason they had for taking him, Steve didn't care. He was in. Soon, he would be a real soldier, and maybe, someday, he'd even be an American hero.